MW01141833

Isaac Hooke

PUBLISHED BY:

Hooke Publishing
Copyright © 2013

IsaacHooke.com

Cover by:
Lars Von Lukas

This is a work of fiction. All characters, names,
places and events are the product of the author's
imagination or used fictitiously.

CHAPTER ONE

Ari sat by the frosty window, and sipped rosemary tea with shaking hands. She stared at the snow-covered street outside, and contemplated a life that was nearing its end.

She was only twenty-nine years old, though she looked ninety-nine. Vitra had ravaged her body, sucked away her youth, leaving a shriveled shell. Like all Users, she was destined to flare blindingly bright in life, only to burn out all too soon.

Ten years had passed since Hoodwink had gone. Somehow he'd gotten his message through. Somehow he'd passed the Forever Gate and communicated with the gols. He'd become legendary among the Users for it.

But the contact had proven disastrous. The gols used the opportunity to lay a trap, and almost every last User had died. Only Ari and Leader survived.

She was Leader now. In those ten years, she'd relaunched the group, and given everything she had to them. Body. Mind. *Soul.* For what? It hadn't mattered. She hadn't changed a thing. The world was still dying and there was nothing she could do about it. The snowstorms worsened, the cold became colder. More and more of the gols fell victim to the mind plague. And then there was The Drop, a relatively recent phenomenon that involved human beings dropping dead for no apparent reason. Not just one at a time, mind, but hundreds throughout the city. Men, women and children. Young and old. It didn't matter who you were, or what you were doing, you weren't immune to The Drop. If you don't watch out, The Drop's going to get you. Don't do any wrong, or The Drop'll have ya. The Drop. The Drop. The Drop.

Society was falling apart. Despite her best efforts. Despite her attempts to seize power from Jeremy, the mayor. Jeremy. She'd had to leave him, seven years ago, when it became too obvious she was a User, and aging at a rate far faster than normal. Jeremy probably wasn't all that happy, given how much he'd paid to have the gols revise her against her will. Then again, he'd taken another wife soon after, so maybe he was glad Ari left. Glad to replace her with a young, beautiful wife.

Beauty. It'd been a curse, in her youth. Suitors had pursued her relentlessly, never granting her peace. Jeremy had protected her through it all, and only he won her heart in the end. He was--no, those were false memories. Just as most of her personality had been false, fashioned specifically for the marriage. Her knowledge of poetry, music, and painting. Her comprehension of politics, social intelligence, and manipulation. Her skills in the bedroom. She was programmed to be his perfect mate.

Only her political talents were still of some use. The remaining skills? Utter chaff. She had no piano to play. No canvas to paint. No one cared about her poetry. And no one would make love to her.

She was alone in this tiny shack of a house, which was a pittance compared to the luxury she was used to, and her only contact with the outside world was through the furtive missives sent to the New Users. That and the human nurse who visited once a day to bathe her and prepare her meals. Sometimes she confused him for Jeremy, and even addressed him "Mayor." The nurse always humored her, saying "yes Ari" to most everything she said. Because of that, occasionally she played tricks on him, or told him terrible swear words involving her most intimate body parts to see how he'd react, but the response was always the same. "Yes Ari."

She set down her cup angrily. *Yes Ari.* How she despised that patronizing nurse. Didn't he understand the power she wielded? Didn't he realize that she could vaporize him with a thought? She'd grown so vast in power these past ten years. She was one of the strongest Users, despite her outward appearance, and vitra literally stormed within her.

Her tea had grown cold. She allowed electricity to spark from her fingers, and instantly the liquid boiled. She took a tentative sip. Ah, much better. She remembered a time when hot tea scalded her tongue. These days it was the only thing she could drink--everything else felt cold. It was getting so very hard to keep warm at her age. So very hard.

But I'm not that old! a part of her shouted. All she had to do was look at the liver spots on her trembling hands. *Oh yes you are.*

A hurried knock came at the front door and she almost dropped the cup.

"I'm coming! I'm coming!" She crankily grabbed her cane, and steeled herself for what would come. She stood all at once, and flinched at the agony in her left knee. Something always hurt these days. Her left knee. Her right shoulder. Her lower back. She massaged electricity into the knee, and it helped, a little.

The knocking at the front door became more frantic.

"*I said I was coming!*" She began the long journey to the door. The shack was small, but so was her stride, and she crossed the room step by tiny step. She wondered who was bothering her this morning. The nurse wasn't scheduled to visit for another three hours.

She finally reached the door, and paused a moment, not at all looking forward to the cold that would come. The blasted fool outside the door knocked again, and she opened the door irritably.

A wave of frigid air assailed her. *Damn this cold!*

Shivering, she recognized Jackson, a messenger who'd joined the New Users a year ago. He was the highly-connected cousin of the mayor. A little on the dumb side.

"What is it?" Her breath misted. "Why have you come here in broad daylight? Were you followed?" She glanced at the snowy street behind him. There were only a few people about. Human.

"Leader Ari!" Jackson bowed excitedly.

"Yes yes." Ari waved a dismissive hand. "Spare me the formalities and answer the question damn you."

Jackson bounced on his heels rather exuberantly. "He's done it. He's really done it. He's crossed back!"

"Who's crossed back? Speak plainly, idiot!" Old age had made her a little crabby, she had to admit. That, and the irrepressible cold.

The man offered her an open journal.

Ari no longer noticed the man, nor the breath misting between them, nor even the cold. All of her attention was on that diary, which she recognized immediately. It was the diary that was twin to the one Hoodwink had taken with him, a diary rigged to instantly reflect any words written in his copy. It was the diary that was kept on display in the New User headquarters deep underground, reverently left open to the page of Hoodwink's last missive ten years ago. It was the diary she'd sat beside for weeks after he'd gone, futilely waiting for a message from her father, a message that never came.

Something new was written beneath the last entry, in Hoodwink's own handwriting. A single sentence:

Told you I'd come back.

CHAPTER TWO

Ari snatched the book from Jackson and slammed the door. She made the long return journey to her spot by the window and plunked herself down in the chair.

Her eyes drifted to the bookshelf hammered into the wall by the window, a shelf whose tomes had made her laugh and cry throughout the lonely nights. Some of those books had kept her warm, filling her mind with visions of tropical islands and sand and trees and coconuts. Others had only made her cold. Pin-prick cold. Much like the book she held now in her lap.

Told you I'd come back.

Jeremy had laid an intricate trap for her. Of that she had no doubt. He must have discovered his cousin Jackson was one of the Users, and he'd arranged for him to deliver the book in a bid to reveal her hiding place.

That meant the gols were coming.

She was too tired to run. She'd run at first, those seven years ago. Constantly moving from place to place. But then five years ago she went into permanent hiding because she just couldn't do it anymore.

Couldn't run. And she swore then that if she were discovered, she'd make her last stand here.

She renewed that promise now, swearing to go down in a storm of glory that would be talked about among the New Users for years. Well, for as long as this fragile society lasted, anyway.

A strange sense of peace came over her, now that the choice was made, and the book in her lap didn't feel so cold, nor so heavy. She stretched her fingers and let her gaze return to the snowy street outside, and she waited, conserving her charge, readying herself for one final hurrah.

After a time, she heard the jangle of keys in the door.

The time to die had come.

She let the current flow through her body, allowed it to crisscross her skin in deadly waves. She looked like a harmless little old lady, she was sure.

But the first gol, or man, to touch this little old lady would be utterly incinerated.

CHAPTER THREE

Ari heard the door open and close behind her. Then the footfalls came. Muted. Cautious. She couldn't tell how many intruders had entered. Two. Three? If that was so, the gols had grossly underestimated her.

She fed the charge inside her, and the air above her skin began to crackle with a subtle hint of energy.

"Hello Ari," Nurse Richard said.

Those words saved his life--Ari released the charge a split second before Richard's fingers wrapped around her upper arm.

"Time for your bath," Richard said.

Ari slumped in relief. Not yet, then. *Not yet.*

She set aside the diary. "Why so early today?"

Richard shrugged. "I'm here at the usual time."

Had she really whiled away the entire morning already?

Richard glanced at the book, nosy as always. "What were you reading?" His features were angular and harsh, his eyes close-set.

She bared her teeth in a smile. "A pleasant fiction about a dead man who returns to life ten years after abandoning his daughter."

Ari numbly let the man lead her from the main chamber to the only other room in the shack. Said room was more a closet than anything else. Without comment, Richard emptied her chamber pot into the sack he'd brought along for the purpose. Normally the residents of Luckdown District just dumped their excretions out the window, but over time disgusting brown stalagmites formed along the walls, half buried in the snow. She hated that. A lot of people liked it, unfortunately. Take her neighbors. They were always talking about how solid their walls of wattle-and-shit were. At least they weren't nosy, though they had to wonder how she could afford a nurse. Only once did a robber try to steal from her. She'd left him with a seriously blistered hand, and a message for other aspiring thieves--this house was off-limits.

Richard undressed her, and lowered her into the small tub that took up half the room. As usual, he'd brought along a water bladder. She didn't have a fireplace, so he boiled the water before coming, and by the time he reached here the contents had always cooled to a pleasant lukewarm. Pleasant or no, today she shivered for the entire session. Normally she would've made some crude joke at least once, but she wasn't in the mood. Not today. She kept expecting gols to come rushing inside. If they did come, she supposed there was one plus to being caught with her pants down like this-- the water would amplify her charge.

Afterward, she dressed, and Richard set out her meal. Today it was previously cooked chicken, now cold, with hard bread on the side. She hated cold chicken. When Richard glanced away, distracted by the distant screaming of one of the neighbors, she unleashed a trickle of electricity into the meat. There, much better.

"Is everything all right Ari?" Richard said.

She chewed on, just as if he'd said nothing. *Chewed*. Her teeth were the one thing the ravages of vitra had left intact, thankfully.

At last she deigned to answer him. "Everything's just fine." She glanced at the doorway.

"There," Richard said. "You did it

again."

"What?" She set down the chicken. "Well speak up you blathering idiot! I may be old, but I won't stand for patronizing."

Richard merely smiled. "Why do you keep looking at the door?"

"The door. I--" Why indeed? If the gols were going to come, they would have arrived already. What was Jeremy's game?

They planned to come in the night, no doubt, and collar her while she slept. That was the best way to capture a User. Without casualties, anyway. Well she'd be damned if she let herself go out that way. If she was to die, she was going to do it on her own terms. Uncollared and free.

She was sick of Jeremy playing with her.

"Richard," she said. "Would you help me with something?"

"That's what you pay me for, dear Ari," Richard said.

She grated her teeth at his patronizing tone. "I want to go for a walk."

He raised his eyebrows and stared at her for a moment, then he smiled that infuriating smile of his. "As you wish, dear Ari."

And so he helped her dress in her fur

cloak, fur cap, and fur boots, clothes maybe a little too expensive for a resident of this quarter, but given how little she actually went out, she doubted anyone really noticed or cared.

Richard led her out into the raw cold. She walked across the snowpack with one hand clenching his, and the other clenching her cane.

She saw the Forever Gate in the distance, looming over the city like an indomitable titan. She'd always regretted that she hadn't climbed the Gate to search for her father. She should have gone while she was still young in body. She should have abandoned the Users, and let the previous Leader rebuild the group on his own. Likely there'd be no Users today if she'd done that, she had to remind herself. Regret and second guesses were dark pits she'd struggled against her entire life. Very soon she'd never know those pits again. A comfort, though a small one.

She saw a small child nearby. A little girl, huddling in the cold. She paused beside the child, and looked down at those weary, sad eyes.

"Ah to hell with it." She took off her fur cloak, and before she could change her mind, dumped it in the child's lap.

The little girl looked at her prize in disbelief, and then took off with it at a run.

If Ari was cold before, now she was positively frigid.

"Why'd you do that?" Richard said.

"Just shut-up and walk me." She could hardly talk for her chattering teeth.

A group of ten gols in the armor of the city guard stood in the square ahead. All of them were looking at her. None of them seemed to have the slobbering faces that marked those with the gol mind disease.

She filled herself with vitra, and steered Richard toward the group.

"What's your game, Ari?" Richard said.

"What, no *dear* before my name this time?" The vitra flowed through her veins and filled her with warmth. She dragged Richard onward, and she could feel him struggling to pull her away. Likely he was surprised by her strength. It was an illusion of course. Little bursts of strategically-placed electricity that weakened his muscles in just the right places, at just the right times. That, and the gentle boost the flowing current gave to her own strength.

"Hello *gentle* men," Ari said to the

gols. She smiled a sweet, grandmotherly smile. "Lounging around in the cold, spying on the citizens, are we?"

She pushed Richard away, and before any of the guards could answer, she attacked with everything she had.

Bolts of lightning flashed from her fingertips. Tendrils of energy sparked from her hair. Surely she looked a demon arisen from the seven hells, born into this world to wreak vengeance upon those who would collar humankind. In moments, all that remained of the ten gols were cinder blocks and charred bodies. Those all-too-human faces wore expressions of shock and disbelief.

When you used massive quantities of vitra like that, you drew the city guards by the score. Small amounts of vitra were virtually undetectable, and you could even get away with medium quantities if gols were far away. But for what she just used, why, guards would come calling from all quarters of the city.

And though she'd used up her entire charge in that attack, she began to laugh.

Let them come.

She was ready to die. More than ready.

But then she had a thought. What if they recognized that she had no charge left? What if they collared her instead of killing her? No. No. She couldn't let them take her.

She surveyed the square in a panic. She could still run. It didn't have to end like this. A few human bystanders stared at her in horror, but when she met their gaze, they ran off. None of them would follow her. And the nearest gol barracks were still a ways distant. Yes, she could make it.

But she needed Richard's help now more than ever. "Richard? Where are you, you imbecile! We have to get out of here!"

For answer, a fist slammed her ribs, and she collapsed to the snow.

CHAPTER FOUR

Ari nearly blacked out when she struck the hard snowpack. Her hip and ribs ached something nasty. So cold. So very cold. Why had she given up her coat?

"You're a User!" Richard kicked her now in those same ribs, and she felt the age-brittle bones crack. *No*, she wanted to say. *You're killing me!* But no voice would come to her. Didn't she just want to die a few moments ago? Yes, but she wanted to fall in battle, not to some idiot nurse beating her to death.

She tried vainly to reach the spark inside her, hoping the pain would ignite something inside her, but she had nothing left.

She would've laughed again, if she could.

Ari, the great Leader of the New Users, kicked to death by her own nurse.

Richard rammed his boot into her ribs still again. More cracks.

"You fool," she managed through the pain. "They'll kill you too when they come." Would he believe her deception?

Richard raised his boot to kick her a

third time, but hesitated.

She heard it then. The crunch of approaching boots. She tried to lift her head, but she couldn't see who came, not from where she lay.

Richard backed away. "I don't know this woman," she heard him say.

Her heart sank. So the gols were here already. She'd be collared, and jailed, and would die rotting in the dungeon. This was the end.

She relaxed her neck muscles. She didn't feel so cold anymore. No. The warmth of sleep beckoned. The warmth of oblivion.

The newcomer strode right up to Richard and planted a fist squarely in his jaw. Richard fell backward in the snow.

"Run," the newcomer said to Richard.

Richard got up and stumbled backward a few paces, then he turned around and hightailed it out of there.

The newcomer knelt beside Ari.

"Are you all right?" He said.

She looked up groggily. It must be a dream.

The newcomer furrowed his brow, and he gently explored her ribs with one hand.

She moaned. The pain of his touch brought her away from the edge, and the cold crept back with a vengeance. She shivered uncontrollably.

"We'll have to heal that before we can go on," he said.

She stared at him, shivering. So many words filled her mind, but her chattering teeth managed to form just one. "You."

"Nice to see you too, Ari, it is. You'll have to thank your friend Jackson for me later. Led me right to you, though he didn't know it. I was going to drop in later, when I was sure you were alone. Shame that you've burned the pals I brought, though. I leave my escort for a minute and look what you go and do. If only you knew how much convincing it took to bring them along." He glanced over his shoulder at the charred bodies and sighed. "Well, there's nothing for it now. Just the two of us, then. We don't have much time."

It was him all right. He hadn't aged a day, and in fact he seemed younger than the last time she saw him, with not a trace of gray in his hair, nor a wrinkle on his face. He looked a nobleman in those red boots and black pants, topped by that green tunic.

An odd costume to wear in the heart of winter, to be sure. Without a coat and gloves, he should have been shivering, but the cold didn't touch him.

There was something else wrong. The clothes fit him too tightly, just as if each piece was melded into the skin and could never be taken off. Worse, there was a symbol stamped into the white shirt beneath the tunic, a symbol Ari didn't recognize.

The number 1000.

Hoodwink was a gol.

CHAPTER FIVE

The heat of rage banished any cold she might have felt.

"Where have you been all these years you hoodwinking bastard?" Ari felt the tears coming. It was almost easier to believe this was some trick of Jeremy's. Easier than thinking Hoodwink had abandoned her for ten years and returned as a gol, of all things. "I thought you were dead. All this time. Dead."

"Ari," Hoodwink said, with a gentleness that melted her old, rigid heart. "I tried. Really, I tried."

He tore open the side of her sweater and his jaw clenched angrily. "I should've killed that bastard." He reached into a pocket and fetched a shard. The five appendages throbbed eerily. She was always reminded of a frozen starfish whenever she saw those crystalline life forms. "You'll have to use your own charge."

"I don't--" She winced at the pain in her ribs. "I don't have any left."

"You have to try," Hoodwink said. "Can you do that for me, Ari?"

Her father was back. *Her father*. She

nodded quickly. "I'll try."

She glanced down at the shard. The creature felt like ice against her skin, and it only added to her uncontrollable shivering. She took two deep breaths, and focused.

But the spark was nowhere to be found inside her.

"I can't," she said. "What about you?" He had no collar that she could see.

Hoodwink shook his head. "Gols don't have the ability. Not in the city."

Gols. Her father had become a gol. She still couldn't believe it.

She heard the distant trudge of boots in the snow. The first wave of guards emerged at a run onto the far side of the square.

"Ari," Hoodwink said. "We can't let them see the shard."

Yes. And the damn thing wouldn't come off once you let it touch your skin.

"Well cover it then!" she said.

"You don't get it, you don't," he said. "Once a shard grabs you, it's like a town crier to us gols. It's practically glowing to my eyes. Doesn't matter how much you cover it. Trust me, we have to melt the thing! And now!"

She gritted her teeth, and rested her

fingers on the shard. She closed her eyes and reached into herself, searching, roving for the power that had warmed her all these years.

But it was spent.

She hadn't a glimmer left.

She shook her head. She was beginning to feel sleepy again. It would be so easy to close her eyes. "I'm done, Hoodwink. I'm sorry. I'm old and spent. I just, I want to sleep. Go. Leave me here."

He stared at her, the disbelief plain on his face, then he flashed that easy smile she remembered so well. "I'll do nothing like that, I won't."

The guards were closing.

"It's not like my Ari to give up like that. And I won't let her." Hoodwink flung one of her arms around his neck, and raised her upper body. She started to protest, but then the pain of what he just did reached her, and fresh excruciation pulsed through her torso. She wasn't sure what stung more, the pain, or her father's words.

It's not like my Ari to give up like that.

He was right. She wasn't a quitter.

She'd prove it to him.

She reached again.

Still nothing.

It was hopeless.

She *was* a quitter. A quitter and a failure.

And she was going to die.

CHAPTER SIX

Ari glanced at the guards in defeat. The gols were almost upon them. She felt Hoodwink tighten his grip.

And then she noticed something.

The pain, pulsing through her torso, was like a current passing through her, signaling agony upward from the chest and into the brain. That current fanned the tiniest of sparks in the recesses of her mind, and if she listened, really listened, she could almost hear it calling to her.

She reached for that spark, fumbled for it, but it slipped from her grasp.

She reached again.

Got it.

She let a trickle of electricity, all she could manage, flow from the spark and into the shard.

That was all it took. The crystalline life form warmed pleasantly, and the heat spread outward from her ribs. The pain immediately lessened, and then faded entirely.

Hoodwink glanced down in shock as the shard melted into her. And then he smiled fondly. "That's my Ari."

"They don't call me... the greatest User... for nothing," she said, panting.

Hoodwink helped her to her feet, and the guards approached, halting in a semicircle around them. Many of them stared uncertainly at the number on Hoodwink's chest.

Ari knew that if Hoodwink spoke, the ruse would be up. No gol talked like he did.

She feigned a sob. "The man killed them." She intentionally fingered the fake collar around her neck. "The lightning-shooting hooligan." She indicated the direction Richard had escaped. "He ran that way."

The gols didn't move. They gave no indication they'd even heard her. Their eyes were on Hoodwink. More than a few of them were slobbering.

"She speaks the truth." Hoodwink's words and manner had changed entirely. He spoke like a man who expected to be obeyed. "The User flees to the south. Pursue the krub. Now!"

The gols didn't even hesitate. They made off at a run in the direction Richard had gone.

"They'll kill him if they catch him,"

Ari said.

Hoodwink scowled. "Bastard deserves it for what he did to you."

She regarded him warily, not sure she knew who he was anymore. Not sure she knew who she herself was. "How did you do that anyway?"

"Do what? Oh. Sometimes the convincing works right well. The numbers on my suit trick them, make them think I'm a gol somebody. And if I believe I'm a gol somebody myself, well, you know what they say--if he looks like a somebody, talks like a somebody, well he must *be* a somebody."

Ari gazed at the numbers on his chest. "What does it mean?"

"Eight."

She raised an eyebrow. "Eight."

"My gol name." He wrapped his free hand around her waist. "Nothing you need concern yourself with for now. We're going back to your house." He glanced at the snowpack around her. "Where's your coat?"

"Don't ask."

She'd forgotten the cold until he mentioned the coat, and now she felt it keenly. She snuggled against Hoodwink like a little girl. Though the shard had healed her ribs, it had done nothing for the pain in her knee, which flared up again, and she limped worse than ever.

"Everyone's going to think I'm your mother," she said in that cranky tone of hers. Everything she said sounded cranky these days.

"Good." He grinned. Of all the things about her father, she remembered that shit-eating grin the most fondly. It comforted her. "Then our disguise is complete. No one'd ever suspect the leader of the New Users is the mother of a gol."

"Yes," she said, the sarcasm oozing. "And a fine leader she is. In her dotage." She looked at him. "How did you become a gol?"

He smiled, saying nothing. Another guard patrol jogged past.

A short while later Ari was back inside her cozy home, seated by the frosted window, a fresh cup of tea in hand, the door sealed up against the cold, Hoodwink sitting in the chair across from her. She took a deep sip, then rested the cup on her leg. Her knee had stopped acting up, at least.

Hoodwink. She stared at him, at a loss for words. He seemed to be waiting for her to speak first.

"I never thought this day would

come," she said at last. "The day you returned from beyond the Gate. From beyond death."

"So you knew, then." Hoodwink nodded absently. "That passing the Gate would kill me. And you let me go anyway."

She stared at him, the indignation rising inside her. "Now just a minute young man--" Young man? What was she thinking? She cleared her throat, and tried again. Not so cranky this time. "Just hold on... Hoodwink. I didn't know that crossing the Gate would kill you. There was a chance you'd fall during the climb, true enough. And that the gols on the other side would greet you with swords. But killed just for crossing? I didn't know. How could I? Besides, if I recall, you *did* accept the risk."

Yes. He'd accepted the risk to save her. *Her.* Why was she hiding her true feelings like this? Was it the indignation she felt over his tone? Partially. No, truth was, she'd hardened over the years. She'd had to surround herself with a shell of iron as Leader of the New Users. It was the only way to protect herself.

"Oh the gols on the other side greeted me with swords all right," Hoodwink said. "But maybe not in the way you think. Tell me something, just what do you believe is on the Outside? What notes did you get back from the Users who went before me?"

She scratched her head vigorously. Her scalp could itch something nasty at times. Another mark of old age, she supposed. "Only some gibberish about sand, and giant skeletons."

"That's outside the city walls, sure," Hoodwink said. "But I mean the real Outside."

She set aside her tea, and regarded him warily. "The real Outside? I don't--come on, out with it."

He smiled enigmatically. "The Outside beyond the Outside."

She shook her head. "Now you've really lost me, dad."

He laughed, and looked away. "This feels wrong somehow, doesn't it? You calling me dad. Grandson might be more appropriate."

She smiled coldly. "So even you would patronize me?"

The humor left him. "No Ari. That's not what I meant, not at all." He stood, and walked to the bookshelf hammered into the wall. He pulled out a volume. *The Old Man and the Sea*, by Ernest Hemingway. One of her favorites. He flipped through the tome. "Look, the gols need our help, but their inner workings won't allow them to accept it. This isn't news to you. It's what the old Leader wanted ten years ago. It's what you want. Well, jump up and down for joy, Ari, because I've found a way to do it."

She stared at him a moment. "How?"

"I'll get into that later. For now all you need to know is, well, to succeed I need someone on the Inside who can track the gols, and keep me in the loop on how well the changes I've planned for them take. Someone who can get to the control room in the mayor's office. Someone who knows the halls of his house. I want you to be that someone. But first we need to fix up your body something good."

She frowned. "Someone on the Inside? What are you talking about? *Inside* the mayor's house?"

He smiled briefly--an impatient smile, she thought--and returned the book to the shelf. He strode to the stand-up mirror by the dusty make-up desk, and with a dramatic flourish he removed the white blanket that covered it.

"There are levels of the mind." He

had his back to her, and his reflection spoke from the mirror's depths. "As different from this one as ice to stone. You need to go up a level before you'll know what we're facing." He glanced over his shoulder at her. "Tell me, Ari. What would you give to have your youth back? Your beauty?"

CHAPTER SEVEN

"My youth?" That piqued Ari's interest, which of course he must have known it would. Who wouldn't want their youth back?

She answered slowly. "I would give quite a lot. But, tell me, what's the price? And don't tell me there isn't one. There's always a price. Especially for something so valuable."

"Oh there's a price all right," Hoodwink said. "And I wouldn't dare tell you differently."

Ari tapped her foot impatiently. "So what is it?"

"Your innocence, mostly. You'll learn the truth the other Leader thought he knew, but didn't."

Her eyes focused on the numbers on his chest. "Will I become a gol, like you?"

His face became grave. "When you come back, yes. But you'll be safe from the mind disease."

"And will I lose vitra?"

He nodded. "Yes."

She sighed. Always a price.

"But there are other powers you can

tap into," Hoodwink added hastily. "I swear its true."

Her gaze drifted to the window. "I've sat in this same chair every day for the past two years, stared out at the same snowy street. A recluse, waiting to die alone."

"Come back with me, Ari." He strode to her, and held out his hands. "Come back and be young again. Cross the Forever Gate with me."

She grunted dubiously. "How? I can't climb it, not in my condition."

"The Forever Gate isn't the wall that hugs the city. It's a token for crossing over to the other side of life. For jumping up a level of the mind. It can be crossed in two ways. The first is by dying. Die, and you'll find yourself in the Outside. That way is a bit of a blow to the body though, and I don't suggest it. A lot of people die for real. Definitely don't want that." He turned toward the mirror, and spoke to his reflection. "The second way is by denying reality. You just refuse it. It's where you know, deep inside, that none of this is real. That your heart beats in a far-off place. That your thinking comes and goes in a mind that lives on the Outside." He smiled at his reflection. "It helps to have a symbol.

Something to focus on. I like to use a mirror."

He extended a palm toward her. "So? Have you made your choice?"

She took his fingers.

Hoodwink helped her to the mirror. She hadn't looked at her reflection in so long. Was she really so old? So ugly? Already?

"Place your hand on the mirror," Hoodwink said.

She did so, joining her hand to its reflected twin.

"You know what you see in the mirror is an illusion, right?" Hoodwink said. "A copy?"

"Sure," Ari said.

"Okay. So what if I told you that *you* were the illusion, and the person in the mirror was the real one?"

"What?" Ari glanced at him. "That's absurd."

"Maybe. But it's not so absurd. Not when you know the truth. Look in the mirror. Good. Believe that the world you see there, past your fingers, is the real world. Believe that the person you see there is the *real* you, and that the person standing *here* is the copy. That's the key to all this. See the mirror for the illusion it shows you to be."

She cocked an eyebrow, unable to keep from smiling. When she saw that Hoodwink was dead serious, she bit her lip, and concentrated on her reflection. *I'm the copy.* Every gesture, no matter how subtle, was played back to her in the way that mirrors did. The reflection was obviously the copy, not her.

At last she couldn't take it and erupted in a haggard giggle. "I feel like a fool! This is silly. Of course my reflection is the illusion, and not the other way around."

Hoodwink lifted an eyebrow. "So you're sure that the idea for each action starts with you, and not the person in the mirror?"

She tapped her foot irritably. "I am."

"How do you know the old woman you see there isn't staring back at a mirror on her own side, believing for all the world that you're the one copying *her*?"

Ari opened her mouth, but didn't know what to say to that. Of course it was impossible, but Hoodwink was right, she couldn't know for sure. There were few certainties in this world.

"That's what I thought," Hoodwink said. "Now look back to the mirror."

She did.

"Let your eyes lose focus. Stare past yourself, into the copy of the room. Gaze at your bookshelf, or out the window, at the street beyond. Let the walls of reality tumble down."

Ari gazed intently into the mirror. She focused on the window beside the bookshelf, and stared, unblinking, at the reflected street beyond. After some moments, she no longer felt like she gazed at a reflection at all, but the real world. It was only when her eyes drifted back to her own image that the illusion fell apart, and so she concentrated on the window and nothing else.

Her thoughts wandered as the moments dragged on, and again her eyes were drawn to her own reflection. She pretended her image was a part of her, and that together they formed the twin halves of some unified whole, a conscious entity more than the sum of its parts.

Gazing at her trembling hand, she realized she couldn't tell if the hand in the mirror originated the motion first, or her own hand. And when she blinked, was it the image that blinked first, a split-second before her? Or was it she?

Was it really possible that none of this was real? That the mirror, herself, the floor she stood on, the very air she breathed, was all illusion? Was she merely the reflection of some distant being, connected to this body by thin strings that existed in dimensions she couldn't see? The puppet of an invisible puppeteer?

She leaned forward, steadily increasing the pressure she applied to the mirror. Her image was definitely blinking its eyes first, now, and she was the one playing catch-up.

I'm an illusion! I've been tricked my entire life!

It felt like the hand in the mirror pushed back. She should have been shocked. Instead, she felt outraged.

Outraged at the lie.

Without warning the surface gave and swallowed her arm up to the elbow. Her reflection stared back in mock disbelief. She tried to pull the hand away, but it was stuck, just as if she'd pressed it into some thick sludge. There was no way to go but forward--into the mirror.

She glanced around frantically. "Hoodwink!"

But he was gone.

She knew she had to press on, but she couldn't bring herself to. Hadn't Hoodwink said that passing through the Forever Gate was the same as death? If that was true, wasn't she killing herself by doing this?

She tugged and tugged, but couldn't wrest her arm free. Exhaustion began to seep into her limbs.

Come back and be young again.

Her heart raced in her chest. Was she really going to go through with this?

Be young again!

Hoodwink wouldn't lie to her. Would he?

Be young.

She surrendered. She slid her arm further into the unseen sludge. The mirror ate her flesh greedily.

Young...

Her face was almost touching the surface now, and she was eye-to-eye with her reflection.

"Be young," she said.

Without warning an invisible hand grabbed her from the other side and yanked her through.

CHAPTER EIGHT

Ari was enveloped in gluey sludge. Sap, mud, mucus, whatever it was, it hampered her every movement. She couldn't open her eyes. Her ears were plugged. She tried to hold her breathe against the sludge, but she realized her lungs were already full of the stuff. She was drowning in it.

The hand still grasped her firmly, and continued to pull, though the grip didn't feel solid, just as if it clutched her through some kind of membrane. Panicking, she tried to break free of its hold, but then the membrane gave. She slid through an ever-expanding orifice and smashed into a hard surface with a clang. She banged her knee real good. The sludge piled down on top of her.

She hacked the mucilage from her lungs, feeling for all the world like she was dying. Dying might have been preferable to the burning pain she felt in her throat and lungs just then. She expected to black out from lack of air, but her vision remained clear, and her mind lucid through it all. Her fingers tightened reflexively, and wrapped around the cold bars beneath her. Some kind of grill, a part of her mind noted.

She wasn't sure how long she lay there, hacking away, but eventually the sludge seemed mostly expunged from her lungs, and she gave two long, painful inhales. After that, she was able to breathe evenly, with only a few coughs here and there. Her lungs still burned though, like she'd run a marathon.

She released the grill, wiped the guck from her eyes, and opened her lids after much blinking and shedding of tears.

"It's a bit upsetting at first isn't it? Shit from one world, to the next. But you'll get over it, you will." Hoodwink towered above her. The nobleman outfit was gone, replaced by a tight blue uniform that sheathed him from neck to toe. The red boots had become black, the hair, ash gray. He held a strange metallic clamp in his right hand, one that had small, flashing blue and green lights on it. He followed her gaze to the clamp. "My own little access port. Wireless, mind. But you wouldn't know what that means yet, would you?" He dropped the clamp into the duffel bag beside him, then knelt and lifted her upper body from the floor. "Welcome to the Outside, my daughter." His face looked older than before. About the same as she remembered it ten years ago. His eyes crinkled as he grinned.

"I'm too old for this." Ari slurred the words, just as if she'd never used her tongue her entire life.

"Are you really?" Hoodwink glanced down at her naked body.

Ari followed his gaze. She couldn't remember ever looking so gaunt. Her arms and legs were all elbows and knees. She ran two fingers along her side. Every rib protruded. Her breasts were deflated pockets. Her hands were all knuckles and bones. But the wrinkles were gone from her hands, that was true. As were the liver spots.

She shook her head. "Not old then. But definitely not beautiful. And why do I talk like thith?" Her voice repulsed her.

Hoodwink chuckled. "We'll fatten you up, don't worry. Get you nice and plump. And you'll be talking like your old self in no time."

She realized something else, and slumped.

Hoodwink raised his eyebrows, and he seemed concerned. "What's wrong?"

"I guess I didn't really believe it. I didn't really understand. The spark." She looked up at him. "The spark's gone. Ripped away."

"Part of the price." Hoodwink said. "Vitra never existed in the first place. People never evolved electrical powers. It's only part of the program, on the Inside. We'll set you up real good when we send you back though. Promise." His eyes twinkled. Good ol' dad.

He lowered her to the floor and dug into that duffel bag of his. He pulled out a pair of scissors.

"You're breathing on your own now, so we can snip this." He lifted the scissors to her belly. "Won't hurt a bit."

"What--" She looked down, and watched as he cut away the umbilical cord that jutted from her belly. He was right, she felt nothing. When he was done, he expertly knotted the severed end. It only hurt when he bent the cord a little too far, and she felt the pain deep in her belly. But she kept a straight face. She'd known worse pain.

"You've done this before," Ari said. "Besides the fact I have *an umbilical cord in my stomach*!" She flexed her lips--the corners of her mouth were getting sore from talking.

Hoodwink patted her head fatherly-like, then he wiped the scissors on his knee and returned them to the duffel bag. "Think of this as your real birth. From the intestines of the old world to the--"

"Yes Hoodwink, I get the picture." She sat up on those bony elbows, and glanced at the deflated pod she'd emerged from. There were other pods beside it, cylindrical, with human shapes inside them. Slime still dripped from her own pod, and she followed the guck downward with her eyes, and watched those translucent, glistening fingers ooze past the gaps in the floor. She squinted, looking beyond the grill that was the floor, and she saw another corridor, just like this one, filled with similar pods. And below that corridor, another one.

"Don't look too long." Hoodwink said. "It's a bit like gazing at a mirror in a mirror."

"You have a thing for mirrors don't you?" Ari said distractedly. "Where are we?"

"A ship of some kind, far as I can tell."

"A ship." She tried to stand, but couldn't. Her legs were a withered mess. And she thought being old was bad.

"Easy now. You've no muscle to

stand. You'll find your arms are a little stronger than your legs, since they move from time to time in the pod-dream. The hands clench and unclench, and whatnot. But your legs, well, other than the occasional kick, you haven't used them your entire life."

Hoodwink wiped the sludge from her body with a towel, then draped a fresh sheet over her shoulders, covering her nakedness. He grabbed a blue uniform from the duffel bag and tossed it to her. "Put this on."

The full body suit he gave her seemed much the same as his, with a single zipper running along the back from nape to bum. When it became clear that she wouldn't be able to slide into the thing on her own, not while sitting on the floor, Hoodwink bounded to her side. She felt no chagrin at being naked in front of her father. It may as well have been Nurse Richard helping her.

Hoodwink sealed the zipper, and as the suit closed, the remnants of her umbilical cord folded painfully against her stomach. She bit her lip, taking the pain. Hoodwink slid two black boots onto her feet, then retrieved a set of long metallic braces from his duffel bag. "Here." He clamped them around each of her legs. "These will help until you have the strength to walk on your own."

She tried standing again. The braces immediately came to life and she stood in a whir of gyrating parts. She almost lost her balance when she was fully upright, and she had to grab onto Hoodwink for a moment.

"That's the way," he said. "That's the way."

When she released him and stood on her own, Hoodwink positively beamed. He looked her up and down. "Looking quite dapper, you are! My shit and image."

She frowned. "Dapper's what you call *men*. And don't you mean *spit* and image?"

"That's right! Been hanging around blasted juveniles too long." His face seemed a little flushed, as if he were embarrassed, and he masked it by quickly glancing both ways down the corridor. "Come on then. We don't have all that much time. A sentry bot will loop by here soon. I was lucky it didn't get me while I was in with you. They come and pick up the dead, or those who wake-up too early. Some of them make a sport of it, and this is their hunting ground."

"On this so-called ship," Ari said.

He nodded absently, scooped the duffel bag over one shoulder, and let her hook a hand around his neck. He slid the other hand around her waist. She had so many questions, but didn't know what to ask first. Didn't know if she even *wanted* to ask them.

So she let him lead the way in silence. Her weak legs obeyed, the tiny parts in the braces whirring away. Her knee still throbbed from the impact with the floor, but it was already getting better. If she had been in that old body of hers, the pain would have lasted for days.

Glowing white slabs were set in the ceiling, and illuminated walls lined with more of the translucent pods. She couldn't get over the fact that there were human shapes inside them, floating in the same sludge that had birthed her.

"There's so many of them," she said. "They're all from our city?"

"Was wondering when you'd ask about them," Hoodwink said. "They're from all the cities of humanity. Or those on the Inside, anyway."

"How many people?"

"I don't know," Hoodwink said. "Thousands. Tens of thousands. This place is one giant inn, except the travelers don't know they've checked-in, and they never wake up."

Just then a siren wailed to life. The white slabs in the ceiling dimmed, and a rotating beacon she hadn't noticed before began cutting a swathe of red along the corridor.

"Pick it up, Ari," Hoodwink said above the siren.

She felt her heart thump in her breast. "Why? What is it?"

"An attack." He tightened his grip on her waist, and doubled the pace. "Not safe in the halls during an attack!"

An incredible boom resounded and the corridor shook.

"What was that?" she said.

"That's the attack." Hoodwink dragged her along even faster. "It's been happening since I came to this place. The halls shake, and sometimes whole sections catch with fire, killing everyone. And then the attack stops, just like that."

"Entire sections catch fire?" She glanced at Hoodwink. "What about the pods?"

"Fried."

Well, that explained why some

people on the Inside suddenly dropped dead where they stood.

Hoodwink was pulling a little too hard now, and his wrist dug into her side. "Let go let go." She retracted the arm she'd slung over his neck and wiggled out from her father's grip. "I can walk on my own."

"Okay, but keep up."

Another boom. The floor shook. "Who are the attackers?" she said, joining his side. She was panting. The mechanical braces helped, true, but her body was still weak.

"The attackers?" Hoodwink spread his arms to steady himself against the latest tremor, and she almost fell into him. "I have an idea. But I can't tell you. Not yet. Your mind isn't ready."

She let him leave it at that. The two continued onward. Each segment of hall contained its own siren, and its own beacon, so that Ari and her father were constantly bombarded by wails and spinning red lights, in addition to those unending booms.

"Dad," she said, a thought coming to her. "How long have you been here?"

He pursed his lips, not slowing the pace. "Let's see. About ten months, I think."

"What? But you were gone *ten*

years."

He smiled gently. "I know, Ari. Time passes faster on the Inside. It always does, each level you go down."

"Each level?" She shook her head. "What are you saying? You mean there's more than one Inside?"

Hoodwink looked at her, and he seemed like he was about to tell her something, but a distant rumble shook the chamber, and he changed his mind. "Never mind."

"Is this the real world or not?" she said.

Hoodwink glanced over his shoulder. "Now's not the time, Ari." His voice had a strange tightness to it. "We got one on our tail. Take a look, and meet the gols of the Outside."

She glanced back. At the far end of the corridor she saw a shadowy, boxlike figure. It nearly filled the entire dimensions of the hallway. But she couldn't tell exactly what it was.

And then the rotating beacon shined over the figure.

She gasped.

It was some kind of mechanical monster.

A steel barrel embossed with rectangles and symbols served as its torso. It rolled on treads. It had wicked pincers for arms. She couldn't make out the face from here, but a devious red light shone where the forehead should've been.

Hoodwink grabbed her hand and yanked her onward.

Her father abruptly froze.

"What?" She glanced at him. "What is it? Why are you stopping?"

Behind, the monster closed. A terrible crash shook the chamber.

When the trembling faded, she followed Hoodwink's gaze, and instantly she understood why he'd stopped.

Ahead, another iron monster blocked the corridor.

CHAPTER NINE

The second iron monster bore down on them. It was a lot closer than the one behind, and Ari could see its features in their grim entirety. The head looked similar to a sword hilt with those curved cross-guards and that central, cylindrical haft. Beneath the red light at the top of the hilt, three glass disks were set into the cross-guards and reflected the corridor with cold indifference.

As she stared into those disks--the apparent eyes of the monstrosity--Ari decided that her father must live no matter what. He was too important. And she owed him her life for what he did those ten years ago when he climbed the Forever Gate in her place. She'd never been able to forgive herself for that. Never been able to thank him. Never been able to tell him she loved him.

She wouldn't make the same mistake again.

She'd lost her childhood memories of this man, but he was her father, *her father*. And that meant everything to her.

She dug deep within herself as she'd done at crucial times in the past, seeking bravery where there was hopelessness, and fortitude where there was weakness.

Her body didn't disappoint. She broke ahead, using those motorized leg braces for all they were worth.

She didn't have lightning anymore.

But she had courage.

"Ari no!" Hoodwink's voice barely carried over the pounding of her boots into the floor grill.

The monster paused as she neared.

Her leg braces whirred madly.

Let's see what these babies can do.

She vaulted into the air when she was only a pace out from the monster. Her timing was slightly off, as could be expected from a body that had slept a lifetime. She'd wanted to kick out, and strike the monster in the head with her braces. Instead her entire body crashed sidelong into the thing. She got lucky, and one of the leg braces hit the monstrosity in the head anyway. She heard the glass disks on its head shatter.

She landed sprawling on the floor in front of it. The wind was completely knocked out of her.

Hoodwink was at her side almost immediately, and he dragged her away from the monster.

It didn't pursue.

A thunderous boom shook the corridor.

Hoodwink set the duffel bag down and helped her up. Still the injured monstrosity didn't move. The small red light on its forehead flashed on and off in counterpoint to the rotating beacon on the ceiling.

"Never do that again," Hoodwink said above the siren, lifting her arm over his neck.

"I can walk!" She forced Hoodwink away and took a step. One of the motors in her right leg whined in protest, and she felt its support give out before she set the foot down, so that her foot stamped. She took another tentative step. Again her right foot gave out at the last moment. The overall effect was to give her a nasty limp. Not to mention that her entire right leg throbbed with pain. She'd just have to manage.

"I don't suppose you have any healing shards in this world?" she said.

Hoodwink remained grave. "Did you hear what I said?"

Above the siren she could hear the rising clicks and whirs of the other monstrosity. "Hoodwink, I don't think we have time for this..."

But he seemed adamant, and crossed his arms. "Never do that again. Say yes. You're too important."

A boom. The corridor quaked.

"Me?" Ari said. "You're the one who's important. What makes me so special?"

"You're my daughter."

"Oh." She looked away. She didn't want him to see the tears that threatened to fall. She pressed her lips together and forced iron into her voice. "Come on dad, let's go." She glanced at the monster she'd smashed. "I think I killed it."

She started forward, but Hoodwink stopped her with a hand and a severe look. He approached the monster alone, and lifted a palm to the ruined disks. He waved two fingers back and forth. The red light continued to blink on and off above the disks, but otherwise the iron monster gave no indication it saw him.

Hoodwink glanced at Ari, put a finger to his lips, and motioned her onward.

She slowly eased herself into the narrow gap between the monster's body and the wall. Up close, she saw that a series of small holes were dug into the barrel of its chest. Numbers were embossed above the holes. There was a kind of a grill in its side, and beyond that she could see the insides of the monster--different colored strings tied together in bundles. Connecting the torso to the treads was a corrugated black bag that reminded her of the material in a smith's bellows. She realized the bag allowed the entire upper torso to turn and bend. The monster could easily crush her if it decided to swivel.

Her gaze was drawn to the three smashed disks on its head, and the blinking light above them. *Don't look at me don't look.* The subtle whir of her leg clamps seemed all too loud in her ears. She vaguely noted that the booms of attack were coming less frequently now, and that the floor barely rumbled.

When she was halfway past, one of monster's arms abruptly shot forward.

She froze.

The sound of her beating heart seemed louder to her than the siren. She waited. The roof beacon pulsed over her, bathing her at times in red, at others in gloom. She didn't dare breath. Or blink.

But the monster made no other movement.

Death throes?

She didn't want to take any more chances. She took a wide, tentative step, and then squeezed through to the other side in a hurry. She spun about, expecting the worst.

The monster remained still.

She watched nervously as Hoodwink hoisted the duffel bag over his head and edged past. He moved a little faster than she had, but just as quietly, and in moments he was at her side.

"Have to be careful when the light on their heads is flashing like that," he said. "You think they're done for, but they still hear things. And they'll strike. Oh, they'll strike." He fingered his side as if remembering some injury.

She noticed a corridor leading off from the hallway. Within, the walls and ceiling fell away. The distant roof seemed made of glass, and she saw the nighttime sky, the stars out in full. Flashes of light came in time with the distant booms she heard. The snowy landscape beneath that sky looked a little odd, and was pocked with holes.

She took a reflexive step toward the passage, but Hoodwink grabbed her arm. "No Ari. It's this way."

And then she saw it. Within that offshoot corridor, along the walkway that led across the chamber, another iron monster approached.

This one was smaller.

Faster.

And those pincers snapped at the air with deadly certainty.

CHAPTER TEN

"Hood..." Ari said.

"I see it." Hoodwink increased his pace. "Can you still run?"

She nodded. She noted that her father hadn't tried to offer his neck or shoulder as a crutch. Good, he was being trained. Though maybe a crutch wasn't such a bad idea right about now...

She alternately limped, and ran, and limped again at a quick jog. The siren droned on.

Hoodwink stayed by her side, purposely not running ahead. He paused beside a pod that had gone black inside, and forced his hand into the membrane, breaking it. Black sludge vomited onto the floor. That, and a human body. The withered person--she couldn't tell the age, or the gender--was very much dead. Most of the muck dripped through the grill onto the level below.

"Help me lay the body across the corridor." Hoodwink snatched the dead man's hands.

Ari wrinkled her nose and grabbed the feet. She could barely lift those stiff legs, and ended up dragging them. The flesh felt clammy and spongy, and she kept expecting the skin to slough right off the bone. She sincerely hoped that wouldn't happen--she didn't want to throw up in front of Hoodwink.

In seconds the two had positioned the body so that it blocked most of the corridor. Hoodwink scooped up handfuls of black sludge from the pod and tossed it over the corpse. Some of the sludge spilled down the dead man's sides and onto the grill, where it dripped like tar to the level below, but most of it remained on the body, the dark, gelatinous blobs quivering over the flesh.

"That'll slow our friend," Hoodwink said.

The two raced on. Ari kept glancing back, and she saw the smaller iron monster easily roll over the body, snapping bones and splattering the insides.

"I don't think it's working..." Ari began, but then she saw sparks flying from the monster's treads.

"The sludge gets in their wheels," Hoodwink said. "Fucks them up. Only reason I put the body there was to hold the sludge. Hurry now, we're almost there."

The corridor looked the same, as far as she could tell. There were no further side passages or branches, just endless pods, metal walls, flashing beacons, and that siren. That wailing siren.

Hoodwink abruptly knelt. He jabbed his fingers into the grill, and lifted away a floor segment. Below, a ladder led down along the wall.

"I don't know how the hell you noticed that," she said.

He tapped his temple. "Smarts! And I got a bit of an eagle eye, I do!"

"Sure dad." Ari took the ladder. Her grip was so weak that she had to wrap her elbows around each rung rather than her fingers, and that made for a slow, awkward descent.

Hoodwink came down after her, and he replaced the grill segment halfway down. The join was seamless, as far as she could tell, and she still wondered how he knew to lift the segment in the first place.

"It's just ahead, it is," Hoodwink said.

He led her down a hallway that seemed, for all intents and purposes, exactly the same as the one she just left, the sleepers in the pods just as oblivious to her presence as those on the floor above.

The warning siren abruptly fell silent, and Ari realized she hadn't heard or felt any trembles in a while. The red beacon flicked off, and the white slabs in the ceiling brightened.

"These attacks have been going on since you came here?" Ari said.

Hoodwink nodded.

"Why hasn't this place crumpled into so much snowpack then?" she said.

Hoodwink smiled. "Snowpack. Yes, it should have, by rights. But the ship has special armor, and heals between attacks. That armor can only take so many hits though, and the iron golems struggle to keep it in good shape. They've been falling behind, as you might've guessed."

Hoodwink stopped beside a sealed door set between two of the pods. Finally, something else besides pods and walls and pods again.

"I've formed my own little group of Users here, I have." Hoodwink pressed numbers on a pad by the door. "One or two are people who woke up a tad early, and lived. People I saved from the iron golems. The rest, well, they're unlucky people whose worlds I ripped away. Just like I did yours."

"But at least you gave me warning," Ari said. "A choice."

"I did. Something these poor wretches never had. I've committed many sins while I've been gone, Ari. More than I care to admit to. Abandoning you was one of the biggest, though it wasn't entirely by choice. Either way, one day I'll have to pay for these sins, I expect." The numbers on the pad flashed and the door slid open.

What awaited inside was not exactly what she had expected.

Not at all.

CHAPTER ELEVEN

Ari entered a control room of sorts. The stars of the night sky peered at her from a broad window, above which green numbers scrolled along from left to right. The floor of the chamber was crowded with small desks covered in dials, buttons, blinking lights, and white pads with words inside them. But it wasn't so much the fancy desks that caught her attention. Rather, it was those who sat in front of them.

Ari lifted an eyebrow, and glanced at Hoodwink. "This is the group you put together?"

Almost all of them were children.

Hoodwink spread his arms. "Ari, say hello to my little geniuses. Geniuses, say hello to my daughter Ari."

"Hello Ari," the children said, just as if they were in class.

She walked forward. All the children were looking at her. Some seemed expectant in some way. Others, despondent, distant. Every single one of them was dressed in a white gown, and with their pale skin and haunted eyes, they seemed like little ghosts to her, the phantoms of those who had seen the truth, their previous selves burned away when they died in that cold world of ice only to awaken in a cold world of metal.

One little girl slid from her chair, and shyly approached. "You're so pretty."

Ari knelt, and touched the child's hand. "I was, once. Maybe. But not anymore. Now I'm just a hollow-cheeked skeleton." Or so she imagined, given what the rest of her body looked like.

"I don't think so." The little girl touched her cheek.

Ari had always thought it one of life's greatest jokes that the face closest to her was the face she never saw--her own. And when she did see it, catching a glimpse of her reflection in a mirror, or in the polished bronze of a sword, she rarely liked what peered back. Despite that most people, like the little girl, called her pretty, and sometimes beautiful.

"What's your name, sweetheart?" Ari said.

The little girl looked down. "Caylin..."

Ari smiled. "Caylin. That's a nice name. I like it. I really do. I'm Ari."

Caylin glanced up, beaming. "Are you going to stay with us, nice lady?"

"I--" Ari glanced at Hoodwink. She gently turned the girl around and gave her a shove. "Go back to your friends Caylin. Go on."

Caylin returned to the desk and sat in the oversized chair. She gave Ari a reproachful look.

Ari lowered her voice. "Why would you do this to them?" she told Hoodwink.

Hoodwink stiffened visibly. "What, set them free? I treat them well. Like my own family. I love them. I do. Without them I would've gone mad months ago. And don't you be giving me that self-righteous look. You did the same thing with your New Users."

"Yes, but at least I waited until they were in their teens. And I had a reason. The young survive the ravages of vitra longer."

Hoodwink nodded slowly. A shadow passed across his face. "I have reasons, too. I do. Children, well, they're growing, and they learn faster. Their bodies get used to walking, and everything else, real snappy. Sure, they all needed the iron legs, just like you. But only for one or two days. When your body weighs fifty pounds, your muscles grow quick."

"What about him?" She nodded

toward the oldest among them. A young man who couldn't have been more than twenty, maybe twenty-one. Half a head taller than Ari, with short, curly hair. Cute, in his own way. Though he had a conceit about him that stroked her the wrong way. And a darkness. *Thinks alot of himself, that one*, she thought. *And he's quick to anger.* Unlike the children, he wore the same blue uniform as Hoodwink and herself.

Hoodwink looked at the man and grinned. "That's Tanner." He strode up to the man and beckoned Ari near.

She smirked, but obeyed. She was no fool--she knew when someone was trying to pair her off, especially when that someone was her own father.

"He's one of those who woke up too early," Hoodwink said. "Shit from the pod right when I was walking by, can you believe that? Lucky for him I was there, because the iron golems were scouting that section of tunnel real good that day, almost as if they were expecting him to come out."

Tanner reached into his pocket, and offered her a packet of some shiny material. "Hungry?"

She was, actually. Ravenous.

Reading her mind, Tanner tossed her

the packet. She caught it, and regarded the thing suspiciously. The texture was smooth, almost slippery, and felt squishy inside. She bit into it, but couldn't tear off a piece.

"You have to open it, first..." Tanner said. He held out a hand, and she reluctantly returned the packet to him. Tanner held the edge with two fingers, and ripped the corner open. He gave it back to her.

She regarded the packet warily. Some kind of gel oozed out.

"It's good..." Tanner said.

"Looks like that stuff from the pods." She smelled it, but the gel was scentless.

"It's actually pretty good," Hoodwink acknowledged.

She licked a small corner tentatively. Tasteless, too. She took a mouthful and swallowed. "You know, for laughs I was going to say it tastes like chicken, but I just can't bring myself to. This is the blandest, most tasteless stuff I've ever had in my life. Worse than piss."

"How do you know what piss tastes like?" Tanner said with a wild grin.

She smiled sardonically. "Funny." She took another mouthful. "You're off to a bad start, Mister Tanner. First the terrible food, then the joke at my expense. I'd appreciate the same respect I've granted you. Try not to be so full of yourself."

Tanner seemed about to reply, but then he averted his eyes. She thought he reddened a little.

"Easy, Ari, I'm sure he meant nothing by it," Hoodwink said.

She had a way of making men uncomfortable, didn't she? But the way she saw it, this Tanner deserved any discomfort she caused, for making fun of her so soon after she'd lost her whole world. Besides, he needed to be put in his place now before he could get the upper hand. First rule of politics: Never let your opponent gain the upper hand.

Her eyes were drawn to the long window beyond the desks. She hadn't really looked out at the landscape yet. She approached the glass, edging between the children. She passed near one boy, and gave him a smile, but the child only stared back with pale, haunted eyes.

She reached the window. What she saw didn't at first seem possible.

She felt faint, and pressed one hand to the glass so she wouldn't fall.

"Could it be true?" she said.

CHAPTER TWELVE

Outside, a landscape marred with dark pits and abrasions stretched to the horizon. The pocked, yellow surface reminded her of old bone. Above, a gaseous ball the size of an outstretched fist floated among the stars. In the depths of that ball, a swirl of gases formed an eye of sorts, and she couldn't shake the feeling that it stared at her.

"Where are we?" she said, still feeling a bit woozy.

Hoodwink was at her side. "In space. On a moon called Ganymedes. That jumbo orange eye in the sky? Jupiter."

"In space." She couldn't conceal the awe from her voice. Or was that terror? "This is the real world? How? Why?"

Hoodwink sighed. His face was grave. "We don't know the truth of it all, but we're settlers, we think. Sent into space to escape some sort of ruin on earth. The pods kept us alive on the journey here, and amused our minds with an illusory world that was quite the hit on earth before we left."

"Are you saying we did this to

ourselves?" she said. "The Inside. The gols. The collars."

Hoodwink nodded gravely. "That's exactly what I'm saying. When we landed, the iron golems were supposed to let us out. They never did. We're not entirely sure why yet, but from what we can tell, we weren't supposed to land here. The trip from earth took six years. But this ship was built to last centuries. By our reckoning, we've been stuck on this moon for at least two. Centuries, that is. Generations of men and women, born into the pod world. Generations who lived and died in illusion. We're not sure, but we think it was the attacks that caused the ship to crash here in the first place. Anyway, there's not enough food, or room, for everyone. Not on this ship, on this moon. That's why the golems never woke us up. If they did, we'd all die from hunger and overcrowding."

"I see." She thought she did, anyway. "So what's your plan then? Obviously you have one, or you wouldn't be showing me all this."

Hoodwink gazed at Jupiter. "My ultimate plan?"

She frowned. There was something in his tone she didn't like. Zeal, she thought.

The maddest and most dangerous men she'd ever met had been those with zeal. Fanatics willing to sacrifice everyone and everything to achieve their ends. "Sure."

"Stop the attacks. Get rid of the need to fix the ship. Let it finally heal on its own. Most of the golems have devoted themselves to the ship, swarming her wounds like flies to a scabby dog. This devotion is partly what's causing the gol mind disease on the Inside. That, and the germ the attackers have hidden in the system. That's why we need the mayor's control center. With it we'll be able to change the inner workings of the gols. And track down the germ."

Ari shook her head. "I don't think the control center can do that. If it could, Jeremy would have tinkered with the gols a long time ago."

"Well Jeremy's a whole different nest of voles, he is, and we'll get to him shortly. But you're right. The control center can't change the gols. We'll make the changes here. But it's hard to see the effect, given how fast things pass when you're Outside. The control center gives us a way to watch those changes. Anyway, the nitty-gritty is, I plan to bring order to the Inside. I'm going to make the utopia we were meant to live in, rather than the hell. And save another world while I'm at it."

Ari wasn't sure what he meant by that last remark--hell, she wasn't sure what half the things he said meant--but her mind was already moving past it. "You want to stop the attacks. I can agree with that, though I'm not sure how you plan to do it. But when it's done we should get as many people out from the Inside as we can, and start over here."

Hoodwink cocked an eyebrow. "You would doom the tens of thousands on the Inside to misery?"

"Well, no," Ari said. "That's not what I meant. We could still help those on the Inside. All I'm saying is we should try to get as many people out into the real world as possible."

"The real world?" Hoodwink said it as though he knew some profound secret. "Never minding the food issue, you've seen the haunted look in the eyes of the children. I know you have. And you've seen it in my own eyes, or at least you would if you looked, *really* looked. So tell me, would you rather live life beneath the veil, a good life, a happy life, where all your wants are yours? Where lightning flows through your veins, and the sun shines warm every day? Or would you rather live in the real world as you call it, inside metal rooms on a sunless moon, where each day is a fight for survival, and within yourself you're deader than dead?"

Ari was adamant. "I'd choose the real world."

Hoodwink smiled patiently. "Real is only a matter of opinion, it is. But I want you to know, as things currently stand the worlds are joined at the hip, and depend on each other. If one world dies, all worlds die."

"All worlds." Ari rubbed her chin. "Earlier you mentioned different levels of the mind, and I asked you if this, right here, right now, was real. So tell me plainly. Is this world false? And if so, what's above it?"

"Nothing." He said it just a little too quickly for her to believe him. "As far as you're concerned, there's only the two. The Inside, and the Outside. Focus on these realities. Please."

A flash came from beyond the window, and a distant rumble shook the floor.

All the children turned toward the glass.

"So soon?" Hoodwink said.

Outside, a dust wave swept rapidly over the yellow landscape, bringing with it the threat of utter annihilation.

"That's not good," Hoodwink said, gripping a nearby desk. "Not good at all. Hang on."

CHAPTER THIRTEEN

Ari braced herself as the wave struck the window. The iron walls rumbled in protest. The siren started up again, and a beacon she hadn't noticed before came to life in the ceiling, cutting that familiar revolving swathe of light across the room.

"Damn it," Hoodwink rushed over to Caylin, who was moving her fingers rapidly over the white pad on her desk. "They don't usually attack on this side."

She saw it beyond the glass then. Some kind of falling star, streaking through the night sky. It struck the surface almost right outside. Dust and chunks of rock smashed into the glass and completely obscured the view. She felt the vibration of the impact deep in her chest, and the whole room tossed.

Cracks began to spider along the window.

"Uh, Hoodwink?" Tanner said.

"Stanson!" Hoodwink said. "Get the children to Beta Station! Everyone out!"

Stanson, who seemed the second oldest after Tanner at fifteen or so, ran to the door, and most of the children piled up behind him. He punched in a code and the door opened. Stanson fled the room, and the children drained after him, white gowns swirling like miniature snowstorms. Tanner, Ari, and Hoodwink herded the remaining kids. Now was the time for calming words, but all Ari could think to say was *go go go*.

Another boom shook chamber. The children began elbowing one another.

"Easy now kids," Hoodwink said. He seemed the only levelheaded one there. "Give each other room."

Little Caylin was the last child to go through, and she paused at the door to look up at Ari. She seemed about to say something.

"Go girl!" Tanner shoved the child outside.

Ari gave Tanner a dirty look, then hurried after Caylin. But before she could make it through the door, a terrible crash shook the room, and Ari lost her balance and keeled backwards into Tanner. The two of them fell to the floor, and their faces were only inches apart. She saw something then, in his eyes. Fear. And something else. Something she hadn't seen in a long time.

"Warning," a female voice monotoned. "Decompression imminent.

Warning. Decompression imminent."

Ari quickly rolled away from Tanner.

She spun toward the door, but it sealed before her eyes.

Tanner scrambled to his feet, and frantically pressed the buttons beside the door. The pad flashed in confirmation, but the door didn't open. Tanner tried again. Still nothing. He looked at Ari, his face a mask of fear. "It's stuck!"

Cracks continued to etch their way across the window.

Somewhere in the room, Hoodwink moaned.

Ari spun around, not caring then that death was coming down on them. Her father was injured. And he needed her help.

Right now.

She rushed to Hoodwink. He was pinned beneath a fallen desk.

"Guess I'm paying for my sins sooner than I thought." Hoodwink managed a smile, though he was obviously in pain.

"We're going to get you out of this," Ari said.

She noticed Tanner at her side, and nodded to him. "On three." She gripped one corner of the desk, and waited for Tanner to grab the opposite corner.

"One."

Though her fingers and arms were skeletal-thin, she would find the strength to lift that desk.

"Two."

Her father was pinned. *Her father.* She wouldn't see him die. Not if she could help it. She *would* lift that desk.

"Three!"

She heaved. The strength came from a part of herself she didn't know she had, a part that was close, yet far away somehow. She couldn't explain it.

Her side of the desk lifted just a fraction compared to Tanner's side, but it was enough for Hoodwink to slide his leg free.

And not an instant too soon, because Ari lost her grip on the desk and it crunched to the floor.

Ari and Tanner helped Hoodwink to his feet.

"Tanner," Hoodwink said. "Get to a terminal. We have to close the blast shield."

"Warning," the female voice droned. "Decompression imminent."

Tanner rushed to one of the desks, and Ari helped Hoodwink over to him. The room shook with the resound of a nearby strike.

Tanner studied the white pad on the desk. He swiped his fingers across it, and paragraphs of text slid by repeatedly. He entered a code.

Tanner glanced at the window nervously. "The shield won't respond!"

"Try again!' Hoodwink said.

Tanner did. He looked at Hoodwink and shook his head.

Behind them, the dust-obscured window cracked audibly now. It sounded all too much like ice that was about to cave.

"Warning. Decompression imminent."

CHAPTER FOURTEEN

Ari glanced at the door behind her. "Can't we force the entrance instead?"

"There's no way." Hoodwink didn't even look at her, his eyes intent on the small pad. He shoved Tanner's hand away, and he began swiping and tapping his own fingers across the thing. "And no time. But the blast shield *will* close. It will."

If that thing operated on the sheer force of Hoodwink's will, she might have believed it. Unfortunately, she didn't think the shield worked that way.

Ari rushed to the entrance by herself and tried to squeeze her bony fingers between the edge of the door and the wall. It was useless. The door may as well have been melded to the wall. She let her eyes wander the room, looking for something she could actually use to open the door. Something like an ax.

"Warning. Decompression imminent."

She saw a steel cabinet off to one side. She ran to it, momentarily losing her balance as the room shook. When she opened the cabinet she found a pair of strange metallic suits inside. "Dad," she said above the siren. "What are these?"

Hoodwink glanced up distractedly. His eyes widened when he saw the suits, and he limped over immediately.

"That's my Ari!" He slid the first suit from the rack. It was a bulky, single-piece costume similar to the uniform she wore, complete with arm and leg holes, and a zipper on the back. But it was much roomier then her own suit, and all puffed up just as if someone was already inside.

Hoodwink shoved the suit toward Ari. "Put it on."

The thing was heavy, at least for one with her withered strength. She managed to slide her feet into the leg holes, and once that was done it was easy enough to yank the bottom on like breeches. The fabric slid over the iron braces on her legs, but the fit was a little tight, and portions of the braces dug into her flesh. Nothing for it but to grin and bear it.

She shoved her hands into the arm holes, and thrust her fingers into the extremities as if she were putting on long gloves.

When that was done, Hoodwink zipped up the back of the suit, and then he lowered a glass globe over her head. The globe warped the edge of her vision, but also had the welcome effect of considerably muting the attack siren.

Hoodwink twisted the globe sideways until it locked in place, and then he touched something near her neck. A mechanism whirred to life behind her ear, and fresh air brushed her cheek. A green light turned on near the top of her vision.

"Tanner," Hoodwink said. "Over here! Now!"

Tanner abandoned the desk and rushed over. Hoodwink helped him into the second suit.

"What about you?" Ari said. Her voice sounded odd in that tight space. Distorted, and full of fear.

"When the glass breaks," Hoodwink said, his words sounding muted through the helmet. "All the air will be sucked out, along with anything that isn't tied down. Depressurized, it's called." Hoodwink nodded toward the cabinet. "Hold on to the rack inside. The cabinet's bolted to the wall. You'll be safe."

"There has to be another suit in here." She scanned the chamber, her heart pounding in sudden alarm. But there were no other cabinets. No other suits.

"Warning," the mechanical voice intoned. "Decompression imminent."

Hoodwink grabbed her by the shoulders. "Ari. You have to hold on."

"But what will happen to you? Will you survive without a suit?"

Hoodwink smiled sadly. "I have to go Topside anyway. But I'll be back. I promise. Tanner knows what to do."

"Can't you hold on with us?" she pleaded.

He shook his head. "Then you'd just get to watch me die up close."

"But I've only just found you." Ari felt the tears coming. She held them back. She wanted her father to see how strong she was. "You can't go."

"Ari, I have to." He shoved her into the cabinet, and fetched a cord from the wall. He tied her and Tanner to the rack. "Look at that. Not even crying. You're so strong, Ari." He said it with such tenderness.

She shook her head. "I'm not. Please don't go. You've already died once for me."

"And I'll die a thousand times more for you."

Her chin quivered uncontrollably. "I love you."

"I--" The chamber depressurized, and her father was sucked out into space.

CHAPTER FIFTEEN

Ari felt the pull of the outside, and if it weren't for the cord that fastened her to the rack, she would've joined her father. The pull soon subsided, and she remained there, motionless, staring into the void, watching her father and other debris spin away. When she could no longer pick out his distant form on the rocky landscape, she suppressed a fresh wave of tears.

The siren abruptly stopped, and the red beacon turned off.

The attack had ended.

When she was sure she could speak without a quaver, she turned to Tanner and said, "I hate you."

"Why?"

She was surprised to hear his voice come from inside the helmet, near her ear, but the astonishment barely registered against the backdrop of sorrow within her. "For seeing me at my weakest. For watching my father die, and doing nothing. I'll never forgive you."

He had nothing to say to that. Smart.

She closed her eyes. *Pull yourself together Ari.* Tanner was the only one she had left. She didn't hate him, not really. She was more mad at herself than at him. Besides, she had to work with him to get out of this. *Pull yourself together girl.*

She looked at Tanner. "So what now? Can we open the door to the hall?" It was hard to keep the tremble from her voice.

Tanner met her eye. There was sadness there. And pity, she saw. The latter only further angered her.

"The safety protocols won't let the door open," Tanner said. His voice had a strange, tinny quality. "Not when the room's depressurized like this. And we can't restore the pressure because the mechanism that operates the blast shield is fused."

She stared at him blankly. "English."

Tanner raised his voice. "We're fucked, okay?"

Ari felt like swatting him. She'd heard enough patronizing for one lifetime. "Would you mind not swearing?"

He didn't answer.

She gazed beyond the broken window. "I say we go out there, then. Look for another way back in."

Tanner shook his head, though the globe around his face remained still. "Won't matter. All the compromised areas will be the same, the doors sealed by safety locks."

"Override the damn locks."

"Can't."

Ari couldn't believe his closed-mindedness. "I'm sure we'll find a hallway that's been torn open, or something."

"There are doors in the hallways, and they seal too when there's a breach. Otherwise the whole place would depressurize. Besides, we can't go out on the moon. There's iron golems outside, fixing damaged sections of the hull. If they spot us..."

She stared at the jagged pieces of glass along the windowsill. One fragment in particular caught her eye. The tip was smeared red. She quickly looked away.

"I thought the ship was self-repairing?" She spoke fast, trying get her mind off that jagged shard. The tears threatened to come all over again. *Focus Ari.*

"It *is* self-repairing," Tanner said. "To a degree. But hit a certain section too many times, and the iron golems have to send the repair units."

"So what can we do then? I need options Tanner!"

"As I said, we're fuh--" He cut

himself off.

"Once you hit a snowdrift in your path, you don't give up right away and turn back," she said. "You look closer, and try different routes, and test the snow, see where it holds your weight. You find the path again."

Tanner frowned. "If you say so."

"You're a pessimist, that's what you are."

Tanner shrugged. Inside that suit it looked more like he bobbed up on his toes. "I'm a realist."

"There's always a way. Always. Hoodwink put his trust in you." Ari bit her lip. The pain distracted her from the sorrow. "Said you knew what to do. Guess he was wrong."

She untied herself from the rack, and approached the shattered window, intending to go out there on her own. Even with the leg clamps aiding her, that bulky suit made it seem like she waded through deep snow.

Most of the desks had been sucked outside, and a couple of them lay smashed beneath the window. She avoided the thick cords that protruded from the floor where the desks had been. The cord ends were severed, and some sparked visibly.

Interesting. That meant vitra flowed through the lifeless veins of this place.

When she neared the windowsill, she climbed the debris, and just stared out across the landscape. It looked as barren and lifeless as she felt inside. Going out there didn't seem like such a good idea just then.

Tanner's voice spoke in her ear. "When Hoodwink said I knew what to do, he meant the mission Inside. Not this." Tanner hadn't moved from the cabinet. "And I *haven't* given up, you know. There's a chance Stanson and the others will find a way to reach us."

"Relying on others is a bad business," Ari said. "Especially when your life is in their hands. They probably think we're dead already." She was becoming hopeless now, too. The sorrow was spreading inside her like a poison, and it threatened to overwhelm her.

"Maybe I can send the children a message from one of the terminals." Tanner waded across the room, toward one of the few surviving desks. The legs of the desk had shifted so that the black cord anchoring the desk to the floor was visible.

Ari gazed out across the moonscape one last time. Hoodwink was out there, somewhere. *I'll find you again, dad. I promise.*

Ari hopped down the debris pile. It was slow-going in that suit. When she reached him, Tanner was already swiping his fingers across the desk pad, causing words and images to come and go in rapid succession.

"Mm," he said. "No answer. I guess they haven't reached Beta Station yet. I'll set it on ping, and they'll get the message when they arrive." He pressed more buttons below the pad. "Don't worry. They'll save us."

"Assuming the iron golems don't reach us first."

"Who's the pessimist now?" Tanner said.

"Well, you did say the ship dispatches 'repair units,' didn't you?"

"Yes." He glanced at her from inside his helmet. "But this isn't a critical section, and the inside door's already sealed off. Repair units won't swing by here for a long time, if ever."

"How did you learn all this?" Ari said.

Tanner returned his attention to the pad, apparently eager to show off his knowledge. "There are manuals in the system. Here, I'll show you."

He pressed a button labeled *Help* on the pad. New words appeared.

Hercules XIXV System Guide.

A sudden, more urgent thought occurred to her. "How much air do we have in these things?"

"About two days I think," Tanner said

But she knew the answer just as Tanner spoke it, because her words had triggered something in the suit, and a sentence now overlaid her vision.

Estimated Oxygen: 48 Hours.

The green letters faded, leaving only clear glass once more.

"Oxygen," she said. "That's air, right?"

"It is." Tanner smiled. "Guess I have time to teach you a few things."

"Sure," she said. She couldn't smile. Not now, not after losing her father. *Focus, Ari.* "So. Can we get back to the Inside from here? And complete the mission father planned?"

"Back to the simulation?" Tanner considered this. "There should be an input on the suit." He examined his belly, and found a small aperture in the fabric. "There."

Hers had a similar opening.

"Good," Ari said. "Then that's what we'll do. Forty-eight hours of air? That's got to be what, three weeks on the Inside? Enough time to complete father's plan?"

Tanner studied her a moment, then he nodded slowly. "Should be enough." He reached behind the terminal and unraveled a cord with a pronged end. "I'm not sure if Hoodwink told you, but the only way to go back Inside is as a gol. Going in as A.I.s lets us bypass the whole human birthing mechanism. You won't have any actual nutrients when you descend this way though, so you'll be starving on the Inside after about three days of simulation time, no matter how much you think you're eating."

She stopped him before he plugged the cord into her suit. "What about you? You *are* coming, right? You're the only one who knows father's plan." Of course he was coming. But she needed to hear him say it.

He glanced across the room, toward the other remaining desk. "I'll use that terminal."

She nodded, and let him continue. When the cord connected with her suit, she heard an audible beep. Tanner pressed something on the desk pad, and a spoken message played inside her helmet.

"External Connect Initiated." She recognized the female voice that had droned on about imminent decompression. "Simulator Access Requested. Allow?"

Two options appeared on the inside of the helmet, *yes* and *no*. She focused on *yes*.

The word flashed.

"Access Granted," the female voice said.

Inside the suit, she felt a metal prong extend from the navel region, and she winced as it pressed into the fabric of her clothing. The metal fastened painfully onto her umbilical cord, and a sudden current flowed through her--for a moment she thought she'd found vitra again.

And then a jab of incredible, body-wide pain blocked out all thought.

Her head fell forward on the globe, and darkness consumed her vision.

CHAPTER SIXTEEN

Ari lay on a wooden floor. Above her, a lone beam of sunlight lanced through a frosty window. The ray touched her forehead, but held no warmth. She sat up groggily.

She recognized her shack of a house. The make-up desk. The table. The bookshelf. The mirror. Everything was as she remembered. Only two hours had passed on the Outside. That was what, a day or two on the Inside?

She noted that no collar, fake or otherwise, burdened her neck. Even so, the spark of vitra was completely gone inside her.

She clambered upright, blinked the stars from her vision, and stumbled to the mirror.

She gasped.

She had no reflection.

She looked down at herself. Her body was very much there. Odd.

She noticed that her arms and legs were no longer bone thin, and the backs of her hands were free of wrinkles and liver spots. So she was still young at least. And well-nourished this time.

Looking down at herself, she thought her skin-tight blue shirt accentuated her breasts a little more than she was comfortable with. Damn that Tanner. The sleeves reached to her wrists, where the cuffs seemed to meld into her flesh just as if the fabric were tattooed into it. She tried to lift the shirt off, but she found no collar to grip. She slid her arms across her chest, scrabbling at the thin cloth, but she succeeded only in pinching and folding her own skin. The shirt felt too tight too tight too tight.

She glanced at the vacant mirror once more. It reminded her that she wasn't really here in this world, but another.

Though it sure felt like she was.

"What am I?" She stumbled over to the chair beside the window, and sat down heavily. The same chair she'd used countless times as an old woman, waiting for her life to end. Waiting for her father.

"So what do you think, Nine?" Tanner said from behind her.

She started. "Don't ever do that again." She forced herself to be mad, when all she wanted to do was bawl her eyes out. She had to remain focused. In charge. "Why did you call me Nine?"

Tanner was wearing a goatee now, matched to a flourishing mustache. It didn't really suit him. "It's written on your chest in binary. 1001. Supposed to mark you as one of the main A.I.s of the system. In theory the gols will give us more respect because of it." He touched his own chest, which had the number 1010 embossed into the tight fabric. "Ten."

"Tell me father's plan," she said. "He wants a utopia, does he?" It was hard not to sound bitter. He'd died for this utopia of his. And right now, Ari didn't care if this false world stayed a cold pit of ice for all eternity. In fact, she almost preferred it that way.

"First of all," Tanner said. "We have to seize the control room from the mayor."

Tanner went on to detail the plan, but she was scarcely listening.

Seize the control room from the mayor.

Hoodwink had mentioned that before, but the words hadn't registered. They did now, however, and stirred something deep inside Ari, the memory of payback long ago given up.

She momentarily forgot her grief. Jeremy. Good old Mayor Jeremy.

She had a score to settle with that one.

More than a score.

She smiled inside.

Her ex-husband would certainly be in for a little shock when he saw her.

CHAPTER SEVENTEEN

Ari marched across the snowpack, ermine cloak worn high to conceal the numbers written into her chest. At her neck was a fake bronze bitch, taken from the headquarters of the New Users. Though her breath misted, she didn't feel cold. She was a gol now, after all.

She made for Jeremy's estate. Tanner accompanied her on the right, and gray-haired Marks, one of the New Users, took her left. Jeremy owned the largest estate in the city, nestled near the heart of Highbrow District. As a rule, the elected mayor always ran the city out of his or her home. Men and women of high office were expected to live and breathe their jobs, eating and sleeping and defecating in the same building where they made the big decisions. He'd bought out three portal traders to secure the land, and blackmailed a fourth. The son of a portal trader himself, Jeremy had grown his wealth by taking advantage of the price spreads between cities. They say absolute power corrupts absolutely. The same can be said about wealth. So what did it mean then, when Jeremy had both?

The latest rumor among the New Users was that Jeremy had found a way to replicate gols, and that he was surrounding himself with a new type that fed on the fears of the common people. He was building an army, according to the New User scouts, though for what purpose no one knew. Ari was looking forward to having Jeremy at the tip of her sword, begging to reveal all his secrets.

Her sword. She reverently fingered the hilt at her waist. Tanner had stashed two special swords in the system before he came Inside, blades crafted specifically for just such a mission. The weapons worked similar to vitra once you gripped the haft, but unlike vitra, the charge was unlimited, and the swords spat flame, not electricity.

The children couldn't just make a control room, like they had the swords. According to Tanner, the children had found the "source" to vitra, swords, and fire, so creating the weapons had been relatively easy. But making something like the special Box that, when opened, would expand to fill up a room and turn it into the coveted control center that they so badly needed, well, that was something the children couldn't do without the "source."

"Why can't you just inject us into the control room directly?" she'd asked Tanner. "The same way you sent us back to my house?"

"Can't," Tanner had said. "The only reason we could go back to your house in the first place was because Hoodwink placed a tracker there."

Three days had passed since that conversation. Three days of planning, scouting, and meetings with the New Users. In the end, she'd elected to throw away most of those plans, and wing it. Any plan that called for her to lick the boots of her ex-husband was no plan at all as far as she was concerned. Too bad she hadn't informed Tanner of that decision yet.

Her boots crunched in the snow, and the sound seemed an intrusion into a night that was all too calm. Roughly half of the street lamps were out, and no one was about, giving the street an eerie, dead feel. Three years ago, the streets of Highbrow District would have been shoveled to the cobblestone. But because of gol neglect, today the ground was covered in snowpack. The houses on either side were dark--the rumors of unnatural things roaming in the night had apparently caused more than a few residences to move away.

Ahead, two sentries flanked the iron gate to Jeremy's manor. The sentries wore long black coats, and capes that flared at the top. She had almost expected human sentries, given that ordinary gols couldn't be trusted for this kind of work these days, but the image stamped into their chests definitely marked them gol. She didn't recognize the symbol though--a curved tooth, dripping blood. The new gols her scouts had reported?

As she approached, the sentries swept back their capes and rested their hands on the hilts of their swords. An action meant to be menacing, she supposed, but her thoughts only registered annoyance.

The first sentry, fashioned as a man just short of the middle years, planted itself in front of Ari. The gol had an angular nose and a sneering mouth. When it smiled, it revealed a set of finger-long canines.

"Vampires," Ari said. "Jeremy's gone and made vampires."

"State your business," the vampire demanded.

Ari lowered the collar of her ermine cloak so that the number inscribed on her chest was visible.

The two vampires looked at one another, and then stepped aside. One made to open the gate.

She casually drew her sword and beheaded the first vampire in a blur of flame. The second had time only to half-draw its weapon before its own head bounced on the ground.

"Haven't seen you do that in years," Marks said in awe.

"Ari!" The shock was plain in Tanner's voice. "I thought we'd decided--"

She rammed the flaming sword into the gate lock, and the metal melted around her blade. She kicked the gate open.

Damn it felt good to be young again.

"So much for our well-laid plans!" Tanner cursed.

Ari led the way forward, sword at the ready. Pines flanked the shoveled walkway that led to the mansion. Deer lay beyond those trees--Jeremy preferred his food fresh, raw. With pricked ears and upright tails, the motionless animals watched the intruders. Something seemed a bit off about the animals. She couldn't quite place it.

When Ari reached the middle of that tree-lined walkway, she realized what it was. The animals weren't staring *at* her, but *above* her.

Swords drawn, seven black-coated vampires leapt down from the pines in an avalanche of loose snow.

She and Tanner set to work. They weaved among the vampires, creating art out of the gols, painting the white canvas of snow around them with blood, bone and flesh.

Marks stayed back, conserving his charge. When no more vampires faced her, Ari turned to Tanner and almost struck him down too--he was nearly unrecognizable beneath all that gore, his hair no longer curly but matted and streaked, his mustache plastered to his cheeks. She doubted she looked much better herself, face smeared in gol blood, ermine cloak splashed with the juices of opened intestines.

"Five gols," Ari said. "Including the gate guards. What's your count?"

"Four," Tanner said, rather curtly. He pressed his lips together. "I think we should go back. None of this was in the plan. It's only going to get worse."

She grinned. "You're just mad because I'm winning."

"I'm mad because we're going to die."

Ari ignored him. She was young, powerful, at the peak of her womanhood, and wreaking vengeance for the crime done to her ten years ago. She led her companions from the tree-lined path and out onto the terrace before the mansion. Two rows of windows fronted the house, and four columns supported the triangular portico that draped the entrance. The red flag of office dangled limply from a pole at the mansion's highest point.

Ari paused beside the frozen fountain at the center of the terrace. The same fountain had stood here when she lived in this place ten years ago, its water imprisoned by the unending winter. Just as she had been imprisoned.

She jabbed her sword into the fountain and the ice shattered.

Three more vampires clambered headfirst down the portico columns.

"Mine!" Ari rushed them, intending to add the vampires to her count before Tanner had a chance.

But she was sloppy. The first vampire went down smoothly, but as the second fell, she slipped in its blood and dropped the sword. Before she could retrieve the weapon, the third vampire

hauled her upright and pressed its teeth to
her throat.

CHAPTER EIGHTEEN

Ari waited for those teeth to penetrate, but the vampire made no further move.

Tanner and Marks approached warily.

"Another step and I tear out her jugular!" the vampire told Tanner. "Drop the weapon, krub. Now!" It licked the blood of its comrades from her neck.

Tanner looked at her, unsure what to do.

"This is where you save my life." She slammed her foot down on the vampire's boot and wrenched sideways, slipping from its grip.

Tanner's sword was there instantly, and he staked the vampire through the heart.

"Five!" he said.

She retrieved her sword. "Well I'm at seven now."

"Next time it's probably best if you don't go rushing in alone. In fact, next time let's stick to the plan okay?"

Ari shrugged. "Sore loser." She gave him a sly smile over her shoulder. Sly, and just a little flirtatious. Though how flirtatious could you be, covered in blood?

Tanner rested a hand on her shoulder, and his voice softened. "Ari. Hoodwink put you in my care. I don't want to see you hurt."

"More like he put *you* in *my* care!" Ari shook free.

"*Women*," Tanner cursed.

Sword held before her, Ari strode under the portico and approached the main doors in a huff. She thrust out her hands and the doors swung open. Not locked, then. Why lock the doors when your mansion was surrounded by vampires?

She strode inside and her footsteps echoed from the tile floor. She crossed a wide foyer. Set at intervals along it, candelabras illuminated tapestries and paintings of underwater scenes--schools of fish, coral reefs, an octopus at the heart of a dark cove.

Wary, she continued to advance, but met no further opposition. Strange. She glanced at Tanner, but he shrugged.

The rising chatter of some mayoral function came to her ears as she approached the reception hall. Ari recognized the colors of the city-state on the flags outside the entrance--three horizontal bars of green, red and white. A servant in white livery watched the door, but he fled inside when he spotted the gore-covered nightmares of Ari and her friends.

She stepped unhindered into the lavish hall.

Marble pillars lined marble walls. Wooden planks crisscrossed the vaulted ceiling. Bright red ermine--white when she'd lived here previously--carpeted the floor. Rows of blackwood tables were set along the far side of the room. Tables not for sitting, but browsing, the counters overflowing with appetizers of all kinds. Honeybread from the west. Goat cheese from the south. Sweetmeats from the north.

Dressed in outrageous silks of every color imaginable, with jewelry dripping from fingers, ears, wrists, and necks, a hundred sycophants milled about the remaining space. They held plates of meat and cheese in one hand, glasses of wine in the other, and chatted amiably, almost oblivious to their surroundings.

She spotted Jeremy himself, at the center of the dinner party. He was like a king at court. He wore a suit of a style she'd never seen before. Black pants and black shoes. A ruffled white shirt, covered by a black jacket that tapered in the front. A piece of dark cloth dangled from the bronze bitch around his neck like some kind of noose.

The servant she'd seen at the entrance was whispering in Jeremy's ear, and the mayor shot an alarmed glance her way.

The chatter faded as Ari and her companions, swords dripping blood, approached. The carefree faces were replaced with looks of fear. Among them she spotted Uncle Briar, stuffing his mouth as usual. He froze when he saw her, and the piece of cake tumbled from his fingers, leaving lips framed in icing. The last time she'd seen the man was eight years ago, when she'd gone to visit her mother for the first time. That meeting hadn't gone well.

She looked from Briar, and at the periphery of her vision she saw him slump in relief.

The elaborately-dressed men and women parted, leaving her a clean path to Jeremy.

She stopped three paces from the man. Her blade was pointed at the ground, but she had more than enough time, and room, to deliver a killing blow.

She mustered all the icy sweetness she could, and said, "Am I interrupting your little dinner party, Jeremy?"

He merely stared. His gaze dropped to her sword.

"Don't worry, I'm not here to kill you." She smiled. "Where's your new wife?"

Jeremy abruptly returned her grin. He could play with the best of them. That was why he was mayor. "My new wife? Which one?" From his voice she could almost believe he was merry, till she saw the murder in those black, tilted eyes.

"Don't you look at me like that," she said.

Jeremy shook his head, as if he didn't understand. His eyes cast daggers the whole time, though he was still smiling.

Ari glanced at the fat nobles. "Tell your friends to leave."

He frowned. "Oh no." The thread-of-gold tentacles of the sea creatures that climbed the sleeves of his jacket glittered in the light. "I shan't do that. You see, now that you're here, well, you're going to be the night's main attraction! My dear, lovely, blood-covered Ari." His murderous gaze drifted over her shoulder.

Marks let out a yelp. Ari spun. A

vampire had slunk up behind the group and clamped a bronze bitch just above Marks' fake collar.

She stepped toward the vampire, raising her sword, already reaching for the spark of vitra contained within the blade--

The floor came alive. The carpet stretched into fingers and wrapped around her ankles. She tripped.

More hands rose from the carpet. Some of those hands plucked the sword from her grip, others restrained her.

Beside her Tanner and Marks were similarly detained. They struggled helplessly against the carpet's iron grip.

The vampire who'd collared Marks came forward and bronze-bitched Ari and Tanner as a precaution, placing the bitches just above the fake collars.

"Bring them to me," Jeremy said.

The carpet abruptly shifted, pushing upward until it became vaguely humanlike, those hands extending into arms that wrapped her tight. The carpet figure slid forward and in moments she stood before Jeremy, humiliated and defeated. Marks and Tanner squirmed beside her.

"I've made a few additions to my household since you were last here," Jeremy said.

The vampire came forward and, whispering something in his ear, handed Jeremy the swords.

Jeremy took the blades eagerly, and swung one about, testing its weight. The metal left trails of fire in the air. He turned toward the back of the room, which was empty, and swung the blade hard. Flame arced forth, scorching the far tapestries.

"Lovely!" Jeremy said. "Though I'm collared, I can sense vitra again, through the blade. Marvelous. It makes me wonder: How easily can these take a man's head?" He met her eyes and stepped forward. "Or a woman's."

He held the tip of the blade to her throat.

CHAPTER NINETEEN

The sword point kissed the hollow in Ari's neck and drew blood. Gols weren't supposed to feel pain the same way humans did, but she felt the blade's terrible heat well enough. Still, she refused to flinch. Not in front of Jeremy her archenemy. Not in front of her friends.

She squeezed her jaw. *This wasn't real*, she reminded herself.

Then why the hell did it feel so real? She remembered what Hoodwink had said about dying in here.

Die, and you'll find yourself in the Outside. That way is a bit of a blow to the body though, and I don't suggest it. A lot of people die for real.

Die for real.

Jeremy pressed his lips together in disappointment, and lowered the blade. "Well, you could at least quake for me, darling. You always did have a cold heart though. Cold heart, and cold in bed. Well. What about if I take this one's head instead?"

He brought the blade to Tanner's neck.

She bit back the plea that formed at the back of her throat. She knew if she showed any sign of concern, any sign of weakness, Jeremy would gain the upper hand. First rule of politics: Never let your opponent gain the upper hand.

"Aha!" Jeremy said. "You care about him. I see it in your eyes."

Jeremy wouldn't kill him. Not with all his sycophants around.

"Kill him," she said. "He's nothing to me."

Please don't kill him. Please don't.

Jeremy cocked his head. "Really. Nothing."

Her eyes slid to Tanner. His jaw was clenched, and he stared at Jeremy with visible defiance. His skin was beginning to blister where the blade touched his neck, and she smelled the subtle hint of cooked meat.

She quickly looked back to Jeremy, at that smirking face of his, and again she felt the urge to beg. But she'd been trained in politics and manipulation. She could get the better of Jeremy. This was a game. The stakes were life and death, but it was still a game.

"When you're done playing with your new swords, Jeremy sweetheart, let me know," she said, thinking on her feet. "I've come to make a proposition."

Jeremy frowned, and then lowered the blade.

Good. Curiosity was the first step.

"You come inside my house," Jeremy said. "With swords swinging and faces bloodied, killing the men that guard my estate. And now you say you have a proposition? Surely there are better ways to introduce yourself?"

Yes, but I didn't expect you to have a carpet that could transform into a jailer.

Jeremy tapped the two swords together impatiently. "Well?" The blades arced flames when they touched. The threat was clear.

"I can teach you how to live forever," Ari said.

Jeremy studied her a moment, and one eyebrow climbed up his head. Then he burst out in raucous laughter.

He glanced at the sycophants around him. "She can teach me how to live forever!"

Stiff, nervous laughter erupted here and there among the onlookers. Uncle Briar laughed loudest, she noted.

"Ari, Ari, Ari," Jeremy said. "Even if

it were true, and that's a big if, what makes you think I'd even be interested? Immortality. Pah! Who wants to live forever on this iceberg of dried shit?"

"Look at my face," Ari said. "Do you see a single wrinkle? Do you remember how I looked when I left you?"

He regarded her closely. "Hmm."

"Open my cloak," she said.

His brow furrowed suspiciously, but then he nodded to the nearby vampire. The gol came forward and ripped open her ermine cloak.

Jeremy gasped when he saw the numbers stamped there. He handed the vampire the fire swords, and he tried to slip his fingers under the collar of her shirt, but of course the cloth was melded to her flesh. "Impossible."

In answer, she merely looked at him. She had him now.

Jeremy marched over to Tanner and tore off his cloak as well. The number 1010 stood out plainly on his chest. "Gol as well. Also high ranking." Jeremy went to Marks and flung open the man's coat. "Just a User."

Jeremy strolled over to a rack of swords arrayed against one wall. She recognized his showcase pieces, a collection of fine blades he'd collected from cities all over the world during his trader years. "Immortality you say? As a gol?"

"Yes," she said.

Jeremy ran his fingers along the many hilts. Sometimes he'd pause to pick a sword from the rack and test its weight. "It *is* enticing, I must admit. Gols can't get sick. Physically, at least. And gols don't notice pain like ordinary men and women, or so it's said. I'd accept your offer, I really would. Except for one thing."

Jeremy picked out a sword and sauntered back to her side. "I'm not quite sure I *want* to be a gol. That whole mind plague business, you know. It quite turns me off to the prospect. And it's spreading faster than ever. Did you know I have to replace twenty of my pet vampires each day because of it?" He rotated the blade in front of his eyes and light pinpricked the surface. A fine weapon--numerous gems inlaid the hilt, and silver-chased scrollwork etched the blade beneath the cutting edge. "You promise immortality, darling Ari, but your argument is seriously flawed. Because you see, gols *can* die."

He slammed the blade into the vampire's belly. The stunned gol dropped the fire swords, and looked down at the weapon impaling it. When the vampire looked up, its expression was all too human. Heartbroken. Filled with one question. Why?

Jeremy slid the weapon free, and an intestinal loop followed it in a spurt of blood. The vampire fell to its knees, vainly trying to hold back its insides, and collapsed, squirming. Blood pooled on the ermineskin, and Ari understood now why Jeremy had dyed the carpet red.

"Did you like how I gave him the other swords there?" Jeremy's voice was filled with malicious glee. His eyes didn't lift from the squirming body. "Tricked him into thinking I wasn't going to touch him! Politics. It's all about misdirection." The body gave one final kick, and then Jeremy looked up. He seemed to realize for the first time that his guests had become suddenly uncomfortable. "What? It's just a gol! He had the beginnings of the mind sickness anyway. Had to be replaced."

He raised a hand, and three vampires stepped forward to replace the fallen one. "Take her and her friends to the Black Room. I'll deal with them shortly. And bring someone to clean up this mess!" Jeremy turned to his house guests, and segued into goodbyes and thanks-for-comings.

And so the carpet released Ari and her companions, and the vampires brought her upstairs, disarmed, humiliated, and conquered, into the heart of the enemy's domain.

The enemy who had once been her husband.

CHAPTER TWENTY

Hands secured behind her back, Ari knelt with her companions in the center of the Black Room, so named for the paint that blackened floor, ceiling, and walls. Only the bronze brazier with its hot coals and the iron desk with its wicked instruments gave the room any color, malevolent though that color might be. The bronze candle lamps completed the dismal scene.

Jeremy stood before her, his hands gloved, a long apron tied around his suit. The gloves and apron were, of course, black. Jeremy held a pair of dental forceps, and he was smiling like a madman.

"You've never seen this room," Jeremy said. "I was always careful to hide it from you. It's my special room, the place I take certain bad people who've done bad things to me. For example, people who rush into my house and kill my guardsmen. Only *I'm* allowed to do that. You understand why I'm mad, don't you?"

"Oh, I know you're mad, that's for certain," Ari said.

His grin widened. "At least I'm not afraid to admit it. There's something to be said about a man elected by the people, a man who embraces his madness, for the people..."

"Elected?" She glanced at Tanner and Marks. "No one would ever vote for this sorry excuse of a man. He fixed all the elections."

Jeremy spread his arms in what Ari supposed was meant to be a gesture of apology, or conciliation. "Call me a perfectionist."

"I call you a liar," she said. "And a dictator."

"Come now Ari, why so harsh? After all I've done for you?"

She glanced at the forceps. "I wonder why."

"Oh, you need not fear, this isn't for you." Jeremy opened and closed the forceps. "At least not yet."

"Why are you creating an army of vampires?" she said.

Jeremy slitted his dark eyes. "Maybe I like vampires."

"What's next? Zombies? Werewolves?"

He shrugged. "This world is mine to do with as I please. It's been promised me."

"Promised? By who?"

Jeremy glanced at his vampire assistants, and nodded toward Tanner and Marks. "Hold them."

The vampires restrained her and her friends, though all three of them had their hands tied behind their backs already.

"I've grown quite proficient in dentistry, did you know?" Jeremy studied the forceps. "Having a tooth pulled is one of the most excruciating experiences of the human condition. It's almost beyond the mind's pain threshold. When you pass that threshold, the brain turns on its defenses, and the person faints. But what happens when you turn off that preservation mechanism? When the mind can't faint to save itself from the pain?" He smiled. There was a twinkle in his eye. "Madness. Pure and utter."

He went to the desk, and retrieved a small vial. He approached Tanner and one of the vampires forced her friend's mouth open.

"A little something to prevent you from fainting." Jeremy casually poured a third of the vial into his mouth. He repeated the procedure with Marks. And her.

When it was done, she felt incredibly alert, and awake.

"Have you heard of the Schmidt pain

index?" Jeremy said. "It's a rating of the agony inflicted by different hymenopteran stings. Kind of a grading scale for pain, as it were."

He strode to the iron desk, and opened a jar. "On the scale, which increases exponentially, zero rates as a pain that barely registers, like a kiss with a bit of a bite. At two, we have a familiar pain, such as a quick, rude pinprick. Having a tooth pulled rates a three, though for obvious reasons it's not included on the scale. The index maxes-out at four, the most painful level. Unfortunately, most of the insects included on the scale are now extinct. But I've managed to get my hands on a particularly resilient species that has survived in the homes of the south."

He inserted the forceps into the jar and removed a squirming insect about the size of Ari's little finger. "Paraponera clavata. Also known as the bullet ant. The Schmidt pain index rates this little creature a four-plus. Yes. It's beyond the scale. The sting induces pure excruciation, concentrated on an area the size of a pencil-point. The affected body part exhibits a totally uncontrollable urge to shake, and throbs with pain for an entire day afterward.

It's like walking over a firepit with a rusty nail grinding into your heel with each step. And that's from one sting. Imagine what twenty stings would do."

Jeremy approached Tanner, and the vampire assistant forced his mouth open.

The insect wriggled at the tip of the forceps. Its legs opened and closed, its mandibles snapped at the air, its stinger flexed and unflexed.

Tanner's eyes were focused, unbroken, on that insect, his face a mask of fear. Ari had seen raw terror on only a few people in her life, and seeing it now on her friend made a small part of her die, inside. The innocent part.

Jeremy lifted the ant toward Tanner's open mouth--

CHAPTER TWENTY-ONE

"Stop it!" Ari said. "Stop!"

Jeremy lowered the ant. He looked at her blandly, as though she had ruined his fun. "Tell me how you became a gol, sweet Ari."

"I--" She shook her head. "You wouldn't believe it anyway."

Jeremy raised the ant once more--

"We crossed the Forever Gate," Ari said.

Tanner shook his head free of the vampire's grip. "Don't tell him a thing Ari!"

The vampire punched Tanner in the head, and forced his mouth open again.

Jeremy was facing Ari fully now. "Crossed the Gate, you say? And then what?"

"No, you don't understand," she said. "The Outside is a completely different world. We're actually on a moon, around Jupiter. On a crashed ship of some kind. And we're being attacked. We're trying to help the gols. We need the control room. The Box."

"We're on a moon," Jeremy said, flatly. "Around Jupiter. Now I see why you came in here with swords swinging. A story like that... it's more than ridiculous. It's preposterous." Jeremy shook his head. "I'm disappointed in you, Ari. You can do better than this."

He lifted the insect back to Tanner's mouth--

"Wait!" she said. "Please. Don't do this. You'll kill him."

"I know that," Jeremy said.

The insect was so close now that it perceived Tanner's lips, and it started flexing its stinger toward him, anticipating the contact, perhaps believing that by stinging him it would know freedom.

She closed her eyes. She couldn't watch. This was her fault. She should've followed the plan, and now, because of her rashness, she'd have to watch her friend die. Tanner had grown on her these past three days. It was too soon to lose him. She'd just lost her father. Hadn't she lost enough already?

"You were right Jeremy," Ari said, swallowing the last of her pride. "You win. I care about him. Please don't do this. You win. I'll do whatever you want."

Jeremy paused. The insect was a fingersbreadth from Tanner's lips. Then he nodded to himself. "Very well. I will grant you this one favor. For what you and I once had."

He swung about and in two quicks steps covered the distance to Marks. One of the vampires forced Marks' mouth wide.

"Jeremy no!" she said, but inside she was relieved.

And hated herself for it.

Jeremy opened the forceps and dropped the ant inside.

The vampire clamped his mouth shut with those corded arms, and squeezed tight so that Marks couldn't chew.

Marks struggled a few moments, the pain apparently not registering. And then his eyes widened, and he began shaking violently all over. Frantic, muffled yelps emerged from his sealed lips.

Faint faint please faint, Ari thought.

But Marks didn't faint. Froth formed at the corners of his mouth, and the flesh all around the lower part of his face puffed up.

"Release him," Jeremy said.

Marks fell forward and spat the ant on the floor. The insect was crimped, and quivered sickly. Marks lay there for a few moments, quivering like the insect, eyes closed, his breath coming in deep, painful-sounding wheezes. His swollen tongue puffed from his lips.

His lids shot open and he let out a bloodcurdling, muffled scream. His eyes were bloodshot and filled with madness. He scrambled to his feet. His body trembled wildly. His head shook from side to side. He hooted deliriously and dashed from the room.

Two of the vampires made to follow him.

Jeremy raised a hand. "Leave him."

Outside the room, Marks' hooting changed pitch suddenly, and Ari heard a sickening splat, just as if he'd stumbled over the balcony and fallen headfirst to the marble below.

"What have I done?" she said.

Jeremy smiled sadly. "Killed your friend."

"He was only eighteen."

"Looked older to me." Jeremy strode to the table and set the forceps among the other instruments of torture. "I have some good news. I've decided what I'm going to do with you and your lover." He smiled lifelessly. "I'm going to be kind. Somehow you've become a gol. I'm happy being human, but I very much want to know how you accomplished this neat little trick. Without the lies, mind you. You said you would do whatever I want? You will indeed."

He waltzed over to Ari and tightly gripped her chin in his gloved palm, just as if he were examining a goat or cow for the slaughter. She could feel his fingers pressing into the bone. "Gols can be revised just like any human. It doesn't work on the mentally damaged ones of course. But for the rest, it's fabulous. I've turned gol executioners into seamstresses, gol whores into assassins. The symbol on the chest remains the same. It's great for hoodwinking people. Anyway, the good news is, I'm going to revise you. Again! Yes, I thought you'd be delighted. I'm going to suck out all your memories so I can view them at my leisure. I'll learn how you became a gol soon enough.

"And those empty memories will be replaced with, well, something fun! You and your lover are going to be my personal fellators. Every day when I wake up, you'll take turns. You'll follow me around my house all day, naked, begging to fulfill me. But you won't be allowed until the next morning. You'll live only to pleasure me, and my pleasure will be your greatest reward. You'll be so debased, so degenerate, no one will recognize you as anything even remotely resembling a woman. And the sad part is, you'll be loving every minute of it." He glanced at the vampires. "Take them to the revision chamber."

"You can't do this," Ari said as the vampires hauled her to her feet. "You can't destroy us like this. You wouldn't."

"I can. I would. And I will." Jeremy walked to the door. "I look forward to many mornings of mulled wine, my dearest Ari, the daily crier in my hands, your head between my legs, your mouth right where it belongs. Ta-ta."

CHAPTER TWENTY-TWO

Memories.

Was Ari truly just the sum of her memories? Or was she something more? Something that experience couldn't change. Something that amnesia, or circumstance, could never wipe away. And if she were wiped and rewritten, her memories replaced by a lifetime in a whorehouse, would she still retain the dauntless spirit that had kept her going all these long years? The love of humanity that she'd held in her heart through it all? Sure, she'd grown crabby, and maybe a bit cynical in her later years, but she still loved the world and its people. That love was sorely tested at times, especially recently, but it was a love she'd retained despite everything, a love that allowed her to fight for humanity. Would she lose that love? Or would it remain deep inside her, hidden away by revision, out of reach but still present, like vitra beneath the collar?

The collar. The bronze bitch was a hiccup in the program, according to Tanner. A rule inherited from the days when the world was based on what he called an *immersive video game*.

"We will have a world uncollared," Tanner had told her. "A world where every man can freely use the spark inside him without aging." She had once thought him a pessimist, but she was wrong. He was more a romantic. Much like she'd been when the Users had first inducted her. Maybe that's why she'd grown to like Tanner so much.

"But it will be a false world," she said, taking over the role of pessimist. "A fake one."

"But isn't the world that the eyes see, the ears hear, and the senses feel, the only reality there is? Isn't what we taste and smell, real? Bits of light called photons shine from the sun and reflect from surfaces onto our eyes, and our mind puts them back together to form an image. Would the world be any less real if we didn't have eyes and sent out waves of sound instead, and those waves returned to us and were interpreted the same way our minds interpreted photons? Or if we had some device plugged into our bellies that tapped into the wires implanted in our spinal cords, and fed images and sounds and data for all five senses to our heads? Aren't all three cases the same? Isn't what feeds our minds *real*?"

"You really buy into this reality-is-what-feeds-the-mind crap, don't you?"

"I buy into the truth, Ari," Tanner said. "And the truth is, what feeds the mind *is* reality. No matter who or what is doing the feeding. The eyes. A wire. The mind itself."

As the revisor strapped Ari into the revision chair, she understood the truth of Tanner's words more than ever. She would be rewritten again, her greatest fear. She'd forget all she knew of the Outside. Her reality would become a living hell.

She'd failed in her mission. She'd failed Hoodwink. She'd failed herself.

It was a small consolation, knowing her air would run out in the real world two days from now. Only three weeks on the Inside, living this hell, then she'd die without warning. Just another victim of The Drop.

Her wrists were clamped in an iron vise. There was a handhold beneath her palms, so that she had something to grip "when the pain comes," as the revisor told her. She was strapped to an iron chair, and two prongs had been folded down from above to touch her temples. Was it the prongs that would reshape her?

Though she'd been revised before, she remembered none of this.

For the first time since she left the house in this new body, she felt cold.

Tanner was strapped into a revision chair opposite her. Behind him, the headrest contained radial bars of light, each a different shade of purple, the hues changing in sequential intensity so that the bars appeared to rotate. Similar light bars lay behind her own head. She knew because she could see the different tones of purple reflecting on her arms.

Who would be first, she wondered. Tanner or her? Who would have to sit and watch as the mind of the other was rewritten? Would the last image she'd have of this life, this personality, be of Tanner howling and writhing and vomiting through the pain of revision? Or would she go first and be spared the anguish of seeing him destroyed?

Maybe the machines would revise them at the same time. But why did it matter? Neither of them would remember when it was done. Everything they knew would be wiped away in an instant. All to massage the ego of the man who once named her wife.

She gave Tanner her bravest smile, but he didn't return it. His eyes seemed full of regret for the future that could have been. At least they weren't accusing. She didn't think she could handle that.

"Power's been low the past few days," the revisor said, wiping its nose with a sniff. "Battery problems." The revisor wore a long white coat with the image of a human brain on it. "Welp, nothing for it then. Have to do you one at a time. Start with you, little lady, I suppose."

"Thank you," she said, and meant it.

The revisor looked at her strangely. "You're thanking me for doing this? You krub are an odd lot. An odd, odd lot."

"I'm a gol, like you."

The revisor glanced down at her chest, and lowered the telescopic monocle that was secured to a band around its head. "And so you are. A high ranking one at that. Too bad for you." The gol pressed a button on the pad beside the chair.

The machine turned on.

CHAPTER TWENTY-THREE

Ari stood on a tiny island of sand. There was a palm tree beside her, with a single coconut hanging from the branches. Around her the ocean seethed and boiled, though the massive waves never touched her island. Directly above, the sky was clear, sunny. A few miles off, the horizons on all sides were devoured by swirling, black clouds.

In the storm she saw her existing memories. They fought and grappled with one another for a chance to bubble to the surface, if only fleetingly. New, foreign memories competed with the old, becoming stronger and more frequent with each moment, so that as she watched, the seething mass of clouds became a potpourri of sights and sounds, tastes and smells, touches and emotions.

Old memories of triumph, friendship, and accession. Of service to humankind.

New memories of loss, beatings, and captivity. Of service to Jeremy.

Pain spasmed through her body. The pulses of agony originated at her temples, and resounded through the core of her being like the hammer blows of a smith at the forge, refashioning her into a shape designed by another. All that she was, all that she was meant to be, destroyed and changed by a thousand electrical pulses fired into her mind.

She dropped to her hands and knees in the sand, and then collapsed entirely. Through vision gone red with pain, she gazed at the dwindling portion of open sky directly above, a sky hemmed by ever tightening storm clouds. The palm tree swayed in the wind.

The palm tree.

Her eyes fastened on the brown husk nestled in the fan-shaped leaves.

A coconut.

Somehow, she knew that hard shell protected the part of her which could never be changed. If she could just reach that coconut...

She dragged herself across the island. Lift one hand. The other. Haul the knees forward. Again. Pace by tiny pace. The base of the tree seemed so very far away. Sand got into her fingernails. Strings of mucus dripped onto her lips. The sand got into those strings too, and smeared her face with a line of grit. Her head pounded

pounded pounded.

She reached the palm tree and looked up. The trunk had grown, and the coconut was higher now. She was running out of time. Had to climb. Couldn't wait. Around her, the eye of the hurricane shrank, and the waters roiled with increasing ferocity, eager to drown her being.

The pain became too much then, and her body betrayed her. She convulsed in sheer agony, involuntarily slamming her knees into her chin. She shuddered, howling like a madwoman.

The wave of pain passed.

She regained control.

She put her hands on the scab-like rinds of the trunk and began to climb.

But the tree transformed into a wall of stone. A wall that reached the sky.

The Forever Gate.

She climbed that wall, and the waves fought her, hurling into her body. She had to hold her breath sometimes when the water submersed her. The rock surface became slippery, precarious, but she forced herself onward, digging within herself to find an endurance and intensity of focus she didn't think she had. The mind controls its own reality, wasn't that what someone close to her had once said?

The slap of a giant wave nearly tore her from the wall.

Somehow, she held on.

But it was hopeless. The coconut kept sliding farther and farther up along the wall, the wall that ran to forever. Her unchangeable essence, all that she was, impossibly out of reach.

Father...

Another wave struck and she was swept from the wall.

She opened her eyes. Her cheeks were wet, as if she'd been crying. Her throat burned, as if she'd been yelling. Her clothes felt damp, as if she'd been splashed.

She sat in a strange seat. There was a strange man opposite her, tied to an equally strange chair. Strange bars of light rotated around his head. He had strange prongs attached to his forehead, and his wrists were clamped in strange bracelets. Like hers.

Ah, she recognized him now. It was Max! Good old Max.

A kindly man came over, and she looked at him shyly. He was dressed all in white, and had a bronze tube over his left eye, a tube with glass at the tip.

"Welp, nice to see you made it

back." The man held up a small stick of metal. "Keep your head still and look to the left." She obeyed instantly, and he shone a light into her eye from the stick. It made her blink.

"What's your name?" the kindly man said.

"Maggie."

CHAPTER TWENTY-FOUR

She smiled timidly at the man.

"Good." The kindly man pulled the lightstick away. "Looks like the revision took nicely."

"You're so nice," she said to the kindly man, feeling bashful.

He gave her a pat on the head.

"Your name's not Maggie," Max said, across from her. His voice seemed stern.

"Who are you talking to, Max?" she said. Max was the only one she was allowed to directly question. "*I'm* Maggie."

"No. You're not." She saw the cords in Max's next stand out, as if he struggled against the binds that held him. Which made no sense. Obviously Master Jeremy had placed the binds there. Why would Max fight against something Master Jeremy wanted?

The kindly man unlocked her binds. "Welp, on your feet Maggie."

She hopped to it.

"You're going to make such a good whore." The kindly man smiled.

She felt her heart swell. It felt so

good to please.

Images of Master Jeremy surged into her mind, and she instantly felt bad. The kindly man wasn't the one she should be pleasing. She lived only to service one man, a man who had been so nice to her, it was heartbreaking. She wanted to make sure he was happy. How she loved having him happy. Master Jeremy Jeremy Jeremy I love you I love you I want you.

But then the kindly man did something that distracted her. He pressed something on the desk near Max, and the chair that her only friend was tied to began to hum. The bars of light behind Max's head pulsed faster and faster. Max clenched his teeth, and his knuckles turned white.

The kindly man was hurting him.

"What are you--" she stopped herself. She was only allowed to question Max and no one else. Especially not the kindly man who was no longer kindly.

Max's eyes seemed to cloud over, his tongue lolled from his mouth, and a stream of spittle oozed from his lips. The skin around his temples bunched up as the dead weight of his head pressed into the prongs. A quiet moan escaped his throat, a moan that slowly rose in volume until it was an all-out scream.

"Please," she said to the bad man, but she couldn't hear her own voice above that scream.

Max Max Max no no no! Her only friend, the only other person who adored Master Jeremy as much as she did, was dying. And there was nothing she could do about it.

As she stood there watching the bad man torture Max, a lock broke inside her, and a doorway flung open to the part of her mind that memory and personality couldn't overwrite. The part of her mind that wouldn't allow someone she cared about to suffer. No matter what.

Without really knowing what she was doing, she went to the bad man, and he looked at her in surprise. She slammed her palm into the bronze tube that covered his left eye. The tube plunged into his skull, and the bad man crumpled to the floor.

Max's yell had faded to a gurgle. She struggled to lift the prongs from his forehead, but they wouldn't move, the ends jammed into the back of the chair. Those bars of light behind Max's head switched colors faster than ever.

She went to the pad where she'd seen

the bad man work at the desk, and she touched a bunch of different words and pictures. The pad lit up beneath her fingers, and sometimes the content changed. She recognized a few words on it, but most of them meant nothing to her. *Regress. Extract. Resume. Cancel.*

Pressing *Cancel* did it.

The hum faded. The lights behind Max's head went out. His gurgling stopped.

She tried those prongs again, and this time they gave. The metal slid up his temples, and because all his weight was on them, she etched long red marks across his forehead. When she'd finally lifted the prongs free, his head slumped forward, startling her.

"Max?"

She tried to take off the binds at his wrists, and it took her a few moments to figure out the latch that unlocked them. Next she opened the buckle at his waist, and he fell into her arms.

"Max, are you okay? Max?" She tried to open one of his eyelids.

He snapped awake. "Ari!" He hugged her. "Thought I'd lost you."

"Max," she smiled. "It's me. Maggie!"

"Damn," Max said.

She heard footsteps, and another man dressed in white appeared at the door. She couldn't tell if he was good or bad. The eyes of the new man widened when he saw them, and he glanced over his shoulder. "The revision didn't take! Summon--"

Max leaped from her arms and thumped the man on the head three times with his fist. The man sagged to the floor like a rag doll, and Max dashed from the room.

She wasn't sure if she was supposed to follow him, and she started to panic. "Max?" She hugged herself, and glanced around the empty room nervously. "Max!"

He returned, and she nearly cried with relief. She'd never been so happy to see him.

"He got away," Max said.

"I'm scared Max," she said. "Are we in trouble with Master Jeremy?"

He grabbed both her hands, and sat her in the same chair she'd awakened in. She obeyed, as was her nature. "We don't have much time." He secured the clamps around her wrists, and buckled the belt.

"Max are we in trouble?" she said again.

"We are." Max lowered the prongs over her forehead.

"It's cold," she said, and shivered. For some reason she didn't think she was supposed to feel cold anymore. "Let's go back to Master Jeremy. Let's get the beatings done with. Please Max."

Max studied the pad beside her chair. "I've only ever read about these in the system archives. Never actually used one."

The white-coated man near the door awakened with a groan. Max went to him, and hauled him over to the pad. He wrapped his hands around the man's throat. "Restore her or I crush your windpipe."

The man stared groggily at the pad, then began pressing buttons. Max watched him carefully. "If she doesn't wake up as the woman I know, I'm putting you in the other chair and giving you the revision meant for me."

The man said nothing, but pressed a button on the pad and the chair hummed to life.

She was scared, more scared than she'd ever been in her tiny, sheltered life. A sudden thought occurred to her.

"Max?" she said. "Do you love me?"

Those words got his attention, and he

looked from the pad. "I..."

"Do you?"

He opened his mouth, but then shook his head. "She's not herself," he said quietly. "She's not herself." He glanced at the man, and tightened his grip around that throat. "Do it."

The man slid his fingers across the pad.

"See you in a bit, Ari," Max said.

She found herself on a tiny island, surrounded by a vortex of memory. The vortex, and the stormy sea around her, receded, so that the island grew until around her lay only sand--dunes and dunes of the gritty stuff hunching to the clear horizon. Behind her, the Forever Gate climbed to infinity.

Her father was here. He'd crossed the Gate for her.

In his hands, he held the twin halves of a coconut.

"Step through the mirror," he said, extending the halves.

She took the broken shells, and sipped the sweet, nourishing liquid inside.

The sand sprouted grass, trees, and bushes.

She looked to her father in wonder,

but he was gone.

In his place stood a mirror. The blooming landscape reflected back at her. Round leaves, rich trunks, flowering hedges, everything reproduced in minute detail. Everything except herself.

She had no reflection.

She stepped through the mirror.

CHAPTER TWENTY-FIVE

She opened her eyes to see Tanner watching her, holding one of the revisors by the neck.

"Tanner," she said.

Tanner rammed the revisor's head into the desk, knocking the gol unconscious.

He freed her from the chair. "Welcome back Ari." He turned away without so much as a hug.

Ari stood. Another revisor lay sprawled on the floor beside her. The tip of the telescopic monocle poked from the gol's eye, where someone had hammered it in. Blood from the wound plastered the revisor's face. More of Tanner's handiwork?

"Hurry," Tanner said. "One of them got away." Just as if he were blind, he began to slide his hands over the desk that abutted the chair opposite her. "I'm looking for the Revision Box."

Of course. This room was sourced from a Box, like the control room.

Ari scanned the room. "What's it look like?"

"You can only see the Box when it's closed," Tanner said.

"Ah." So she did as Tanner did, and glided her fingers across the desk beside her, and over the strange levers and dials, and above and around the revision chair. She moved forward to search behind the chair, and the toe of her boot stubbed an invisible object on the floor. Like a street mummer she was able to outline the shape of an unseen chest. Made of wood, she thought, judging from the grainy texture. The lid seemed open.

"Found it," she said, feeling a swell of pride at having discovered the Box first. She really did enjoy winning.

She closed the lid.

Instantly the fabric of reality stretched and folded, and the revision chairs, the desks and everything else warped along that fabric, twisting into the invisible box as if the entire chamber were some tapestry that a giant nostril inhaled. The whole room seemed to whip right through her body, and she felt strange inside, *unreal*.

Then it was done. Only bare walls, ceiling and floor were left, with not a piece of furniture in sight save for the sealed wooden chest at Ari's feet.

That strange feeling inside her worsened all of a sudden, and she keeled over and threw up.

"Forgot to tell you." Tanner came up beside her. "It's best to close the Box from behind."

"Great." She wiped her hand across her lips, and swallowed the acrid taste from her mouth. She hated throwing up.

Ari turned the key that sat in the lock of the chest, pocketed it, and scooped the Box under one arm. "Surprisingly light."

"Or you're surprisingly strong." Tanner smiled ironically. "Like a gol maybe?"

Ari and Tanner dashed into the adjoining room, which was empty save for two ladderback chairs set against the wall. The two of them crossed to the corridor beyond.

Here the walls were white, and arches embossed with carvings of sea creatures decorated the doorways of the side chambers. A gold-rimmed red carpet ran along the center of the floor. Triple-pronged candelabras were set every five paces.

"Which way?" Tanner said.

She ran the blueprint of the house through her mind, the house she'd lived and walked through so many times in her early twenties. Urgent footfalls and shouts echoed from somewhere ahead.

"Ari." Tanner's voice cut with impatience. "Which way?"

When she didn't answer, Tanner took a step forward.

Ari shot out a hand and blocked him. She glanced downward, indicating the gold-trimmed carpet. "What's really a carpet, and what's something else? This way."

Ari dashed forward, taking care to run along the bare floor between carpet and wall. Tanner followed in single-file behind her.

On the far side of the corridor four vampires rounded the bend at a sprint. They spotted Ari and Tanner and gave a hoot. Two of them held fire swords, *their* fire swords, and the blades glowed a molten red.

"Ari..." Tanner's voice drifted to her.

She spun into a side hall as flames roared from those blades. Tanner jostled into her, the back of his uniform singed.

Ari raced down the corridor, and on the right side the hallway opened onto a flight of wooden stairs--the back route the servants used.

Ari took the stairs three at a time. At the bottom, she turned into the kitchen, and hurried through the hanging pots and pans.

There were no cooks here, not at this hour.

"The back door is just this way," she said.

"Why do houses always put their back doors in the kitchen?" Tanner said.

Ari ignored the comment, because just ahead seven vampires guarded the door.

CHAPTER TWENTY-SIX

Ari immediately backtracked.

The other pursuing vampires burst into the far side of the kitchen. The fire swords flared in the grips of the two at the front.

Ari turned into the pantry, and raced past the foodstuffs and out into main dining hall. She edged by the blackwood table and out into a hallway that was much the same as the one on the second floor, absent the carpet.

Tanner panted beside her, and behind she heard the footfalls of vampires, growing in volume. It was an eerie sound, the clatter of claws against marble, and she knew that some of the vampires had broken ahead of the pack and were running on all fours.

She and Tanner burst into the empty reception hall. She dashed obliquely toward the sword rack, taking a circuit around the carpet.

The pursuing vampires simply cut across the carpet, and were almost upon her and Tanner.

The rack with its showcase swords lay just ahead.

"Catch!" As she ran, she tossed the Revision Box to Tanner--

She leapt toward the rack, somersaulting over it--

Grabbed two swords from the rack in midair--

And landed on the other side.

She pivoted.

Tanner had vaulted over the rack as well, and two vampires leaped after him in pursuit.

She brought the swords about in a wide arc. Tanner stooped, and she cut the two vampires in half before they touched the ground.

Two more approached around the rack and she made short work of them.

She saw a bright ball of flame at the periphery of her vision--

She leaped toward the wall, and used it to slingshot into the air--

Flames streamed past below her--

She landed beside the vampire and its stolen fire sword.

A jab, a parry, a slash, and she'd severed the hand holding the blade.

A spin of the body, followed by a wide backstab, and she plunged her second sword into its heart.

She hooked her boot into the hilt of the dropped fire sword, kicked the blade to eye level, and swapped one of her blades for that one. She immediately felt the spark of vitra inside her, jolting up her arm from the weapon.

It felt good.

Another stream of flame cut toward her--

She parried with the fire blade--

Batting away the flames in a half-sphere around her that singed her hair.

Two quick steps and a sideways leap from a pillar brought her to the vampire in question, and after a quick exchange of feints and stabs, she'd taken its head, and the other fire sword.

More vampires closed...

She released the spark of vitra from the blades as she fought, launching hell-fire on all sides. She weaved, a dancer at play. Her rhythm was the blade and its fire, her music the gush of blood and the sizzle of flesh and the screams of the dying. She avoided the carpet the entire time, though sometimes her foot brushed its edge.

When it was done, and the vampires lay around her in various states of mutilation and ash, she tossed one of the fire blades to

Tanner, who'd wisely flattened himself
against the wall and given her room to fight.

"Nice," Tanner said. There seemed a
touch of awe in his voice. Or at least respect.

"Well that's that." Ari felt immensely
proud of herself. She'd barely broken a
sweat. "I think I'm at twenty."

"Let's just go." Tanner seemed
weary.

She took the Revision Box from him,
and hoisted it over her shoulder.

The carpet began to writhe beside
them. Tentacles formed, reaching for their
feet.

"Out of here!" Tanner turned to run
along the space between carpet and wall.

"No!" Ari released a surge of flame,
and the tentacles instantly retreated. "We
have to get the Control Room Box."

Shrieks and howls came from her
left. Vampires flowed down the wide,
branching stairs that led to the second level.
Fifty vampires. A hundred.

"Ari..." Tanner laid a hand on her
arm.

Still more vampires came down
those stairs, the gols crowded so close
together as to resemble a single entity, like
the black python she'd seen at the circus as a

child. A giant version of it anyway.

"They'll be time to get the Control Room Box another day," Tanner said. "We've done what we came here to do. We've planted the tracker."

Even more vampires came, and crowded down the stairs behind the others. Far more than Ari and Tanner could handle on their own, even with the swords.

A tendril hurled at her from the carpet--

She ducked--

The tendril slammed into the wall, leaving cracks.

She released another stream of flame into the carpet. The fire blackened the surface where it struck, and the creature squealed, retreating.

"Ari let's go!" Tanner said.

But she was already running past him.

And so Ari and Tanner ran from the mayor's house with death in pursuit. One or two vampires occasionally hindered their progress, but the pair cut them down easily enough. Across the grounds the two dashed, through the damaged gates, and out into the night.

But they would not escape so easily.

The army of vampires pursued the entire way, and followed the pair onto the lamp-lit street beyond. The faster ones ran across the snowpack on all fours, while the more agile ones leaped between the rooftops of the houses beside them, sending snow sliding down onto the street.

Though she inhabited the body of a gol, she was getting tired. Beside her, Tanner wasn't faring much better. Both of them were winded. They couldn't keep this up for much longer. The Revision Box was getting heavier and heavier on her shoulder. The sword felt like lead.

She had an idea. It was a small hope, but a hope was a hope no matter how tiny.

"Hold them off," she said.

"What?" Tanner's voice exuded incredulity above the exhaustion.

"Do it." She halted on the snowpack, and dropped the chest.

"Hope you know what you're doing," Tanner said, lifting the blade.

CHAPTER TWENTY-SEVEN

Ari spun around, and was forced to slay two vampires at the head of the pack. As Tanner defended against the others, she raised the sword over the box and let the vitra accumulate, but she didn't release it. The blade glowed molten, and shook with the power of pent-up flames. The smoke plumes rose to engulf her hands. Her fingers burned, but there was nothing for it. She needed to put on the biggest show she could manage.

The biggest show of her life.

"Halt, scum!" she shouted, her breath misting. The vampires at the forefront had begun to overwhelm Tanner, and he retreated toward her. "Halt or I'll destroy the Box! Halt I said!"

The vampires began to obey, one by one, and the onslaught slowed as the gols in the forefront held back those behind. Vampires occasionally broke through, but Tanner hacked them down.

The vampires formed a tentative half-circle, which quickly became a full circle as more and more vampires arrived. Tanner patrolled that tight circle, brandishing his flaming weapon, forcing back those who came too near.

The vampires in the forefront snarled, and snapped at the air with their teeth. They reminded her of chained curs.

Ari raised the blade higher, and accumulated even more vitra in the blade. The sword rumbled, and the smoke poured forth even more profusely. She could feel the heat over her whole body, and the snowpack below her began to melt. The air smelled of cooked meat, and the pain she felt in her hands bordered on indescribable. But she was a gol, and she'd discovered that she could ignore that pain.

"Go ahead," she said through gritted teeth. "Attack. By the time you touch me, your mayor's precious Revision Box will be ashes. I guarantee you."

There was a commotion among the enemy, and the ranks rippled as a huge vampire shoved its way to the front. This one towered three heads above Ari, and it had four arms, two in the usual place, and two more midway the ribs. Each hand held a scimitar.

The huge vampire bared its teeth in a rictus of hate, and those finger-long fangs pricked the air.

It stepped toward Ari.

Tanner lifted his fire blade to Fourarms' throat.

"Tanner wait," Ari said.

Fourarms glanced at Tanner as if he were a fly. A maggot. The heat from Tanner's blade didn't even touch its throat. She saw no scoring. No blistering.

Fourarms glared at Ari for a long moment, then turned its head and spat some guttural words at the others. The vampires seemed reluctant to obey at first, but Fourarms spat the strange words again, and the others slowly dispersed.

Fourarms glowered at her a while longer. "We will meet again."

The giant vampire batted Tanner's sword aside and sprinted after the others. It sheathed its four blades in mechanical sequence, and then hunched to run on all six appendages, seeming very much like an insect in the dark.

Ari watched the horde vanish into the night, and she wondered what the citizens barricaded within their houses and observing from their windows thought of the whole bizarre proceeding.

Well, there'd certainly be news for the criers tomorrow.

"Twenty-seven," Tanner said, gazing at the dead. "To your twenty."

"You win." She released vitra and the sword went out. She sat down--collapsed, really--onto the chest, and unwrapped her blackened fingers from the hilt. To her disgust, some of her skin remained glued to the haft, and it stretched away from her palms like gauze. Her hands were ruined.

"Take it easy there. Easy!" Tanner helped free her hands from the hilt, and then he bound her palms in fabric ripped from the cloaks of the dead vampires. She kept a wary eye out while he worked.

"Tanner," she said.

"Mmm?"

This was hard, but it needed to be said. "Sorry for all the times I've been a bitch to you."

He laughed, just a little. "You've never been a bitch to me Ari."

"No, I have." She looked at him and smiled sadly. "And I shouldn't have. I'll try to be less of a bitch in the future, okay?"

He shook his head. "Okay Ari. Okay. You're too hard on yourself."

She shrugged. "Maybe. But I can be too hard on others, too. The hammer of the forge inside me won't back down sometimes, and it hurts the people I care about the most."

"Oh don't you worry, I have a shield, Ari," Tanner said. "Made of crazy-strong bronze. It's a little battered, sure, but it's never let me down yet." He tied off the last of the makeshift bandages, and stood. "That should do it."

She clambered to her feet, and blinked the sudden stars away. She didn't protest when Tanner bent to heft the box from the melted snowpack and over his shoulder.

So it was done. The tracker was planted, and she'd escaped from the heart of darkness, from the domain of the only man she feared in this world. She hadn't been afraid of him earlier today. But she was afraid of him now. More than anything. But fear was good. The fire sword had made her cocky. Lesson learned. She'd think twice before throwing away well-laid plans again.

She felt both utterly relieved, and utterly drained. Still, as she walked along the snowpack, she and Tanner kept their weapons out. Her sword was painful and awkward to grip, but there was nothing for it. Some of the vampires had remained behind, and followed in the shadows. Both of them knew it. She'd have to take a roundabout route to the hideaway, and perhaps arrange an ambush along the way.

"I believe it's time we set up a meeting with The Dwarf," Tanner said.

She raised her eyebrows. "The Dwarf?"

"Yes." Tanner glanced at her. "The children restored his connection a few months back."

"And what's that supposed to mean?"

Tanner rested a gentle hand on her shoulder. "The Dwarf's the only one who can talk to your father."

EPILOGUE

Looking down from the balcony, Jeremy surveyed the clean-up of his reception hall. Some of the black-liveried servants mopped the blood and soot marks from the marble, others piled the mutilated bodies into barrows, while still others hauled the bodies away for burning in the kitchens. Some servants took down the ruined paintings. Some repaired the cracks in the walls.

Ari. She'd pay for all this, he promised. Killing his vampires. Interrupting his dinner party. Messing up his reception hall. Stealing his Revision Box. Oh, she'd pay.

"You three!" he called down to the seamstresses he'd hired to cover the burn marks in his precious Living Carpet. "Careful now... that rug is worth more than your miserable hides combined! Make a mistake and you'll never sew again, I swear it!" There was no real damage the seamstresses could do to the thing, of course, other than make it look even uglier. The women were merely a convenient outlet for his rage. Still, fear would make them work with more care and diligence. Fear. His favorite spur.

With a sigh, he left the balcony and returned to his room. He hardly noticed the luxury around him anymore. The tapestries of the underwater cities he'd dreamed about. The sculptures of sea creatures. The miniature coral reefs. All commissioned for outrageous fees. Art that fed his obsession. Art based on water. Water. The one thing this world lacked in profusion. *Blast this icy place!*

Ah well, he wasn't here to brood on ice, art, or women. He glanced at the clock on his hearth. Three o'clock. Right on time.

He went to the mirror on the far side of the bed chamber, knelt on one knee, and inclined his head. The thread-of-gold tentacle on his sleeve caught the light.

"Master," he said.

When he looked up, the dark shape that called itself One lurked within the mirror, near the bed. It might pass as human in that black robe, with its face hidden in the shadow of the hood. But it was not human.

As usual, Jeremy felt the undeniable fervor that accompanied the Great One's appearance, a fervor that nearly overcame him. He could have wept, shouted for joy, and laughed maniacally, all at the same time.

He resisted the urge to turn around. The Great One resided in the mirror, *his* mirror, and nowhere else.

Nowhere else.

The thought filled him with ecstasy. Exclusivity. Such a drug.

Those unseen lips spoke to him in a baritone that was too low to belong to any man. "Status update." The voice came from behind Jeremy, and again he had to resist the urge to look. He'd embarrassed himself far too many times doing that.

"I've created ten thousand of the new gols, as you commanded, Great One, and garrisoned them throughout the city, near the portal hops. They are ready to march at your order. The unit leaders have been assigned, the instructions uploaded."

"Excellent," the Great One said. "I am pleased."

Jeremy felt his heart leap. "May I have my reward, then?"

"Not yet."

Jeremy lowered his eyes. It wasn't fair. But he couldn't say that. Not to the Great One.

The voice assumed a strange

inflection. "Have there been... difficulties?" It sounded almost accusing.

"No, master," Jeremy said, maybe a little too quickly, and he twisted his lips at the sudden distaste in his mouth. "No difficulties at all."

"Good," the Great One said. "Because if there were difficulties, and you didn't tell me..."

Jeremy put on his best smile, and he looked right into the darkness of that face. "All is going according to plan, Great One."

He gazed into that black hood for as long as he dared, and then lowered his eyes. When he glanced up again, the Great One was gone.

Jeremy giggled, and spoke to the empty air. "All according to *my* plan, that is!"

This is the end of Book II.
The Forever Gate III is coming.
Look for it February, 2013.

Postpartum

If you loved this book, please consider leaving a comment on Goodreads here:

http://www.goodreads.com/book/show/17203160

Or Amazon here:

http://amzn.to/VwPNJK

(Or just search for The Forever Gate 2 on each site)

I read *every single review*, and your comments help guide future works. Comments and reviews allow readers to discover indie authors, so if you want others to enjoy *The Forever Gate 2* as you have, don't be shy about leaving a short note!

Thanks in advance.

Keeping In Touch

You can keep in touch with me or my writing through one—or all—of the following means:

Twitter: @IsaacHooke

Facebook: http://fb.me/authorisaachooke

Goodreads: http://goodreads.com/isaachooke

My website: http://isaachooke.com

My email: isaac@isaachooke.com

Don't be shy about emails, I love getting them, and try to respond to everyone!

Thanks again for reading *The Forever Gate 2*, and I look forward to having you along for Book III.

CPSIA information can be obtained at www.ICGtesting.com
Printed in the USA
LVOW10s0929030714

392724LV00026BA/622/P